Dragon School: First Flight

Dragon School

Sarah K. L. Wilson

Published by Sarah K. L. Wilson, 2017.

This is a work of fiction. Similarities to real people, places, or events are entirely coincidental.

DRAGON SCHOOL: FIRST FLIGHT

First edition. November 9, 2017.

Written by Sarah K. L. Wilson.

Chapter One

THE BEST PART ABOUT dragon school is choosing your dragon. It's the part that everyone talks about and the part that they'll tell stories to their children and children's children about someday – if they live that long. Dragon Riders don't live very long. Not that that bothers anyone. If anything, it just makes more of us desperate to live to ride a dragon as one of the Dominion Sky People.

The best part about choosing your dragon is that you join a Dominion Color when you choose. Dragons only come in a few colors, and the color you choose determines your role for the rest of your life – short or long – as a Dragon Rider.

I want to join a Dominion Color and gain a purpose in life. No one wants a cripple like me to do anything except stay out of the way but I'm going to show them that I stand just as much chance as everyone else.

We were clustered on the edge of the towering cliffs, shivering like a clutch of baby chicks. The wind whirled over the black rock of the cliff, blasting us towards the cliff's ragged edge. Did it expect us to leap and fly like the dragons housed here? Towering high above us, in sweeping arcs and swirling inlays, the Dragons' cotes were as intimidating as the legends of the great beasts. These weren't even the grand Dominion Cotes - only Dragon School cotes - but already I felt awed by the sheer size and scope of them.

Our instructor, Grandis Dantriet, strode in front of us, hands clasped behind him, his gnarled muscles bunched under leather straps and flowing silk scarves. He wore his white hair in the Dragon Rider way – long with tight braids mixed between the stray strands.

"Today you choose your dragon. Make no mistake: this choice will define you."

A stir went through our ranks at his words. I glanced beside me to a girl with silver-blonde hair and a wispy sky-silk dress. She was high nobility at the very least and her cold glare told me that she didn't care for my attention. Likely, she'd be among those who chose first. The wealthy and powerful were given the first pick of the newly caught dragons. I didn't even need to guess who would choose last – me. And with my luck, I'd get a surly swamp-colored dragon covered in warts with breath as bad as a garbage heap. If I did, I'd still be grateful. I was here to ride a dragon, not to look pretty doing it.

I adjusted my crutch and watched with interest as Grandis Dantriet took a piece of chalk and wrote our names on a board between the alcoves. Beside each name was a black blank. Those blanks were about to be filled with dragon names. I felt my heart speed up. Even knowing I'd be last to choose, even knowing I'd get the worst of the draw, I still couldn't help but feel the electric excitement of the moment. I was about to choose a dragon. I was going to be a Dragon Rider.

Grandis Dantriet took a curving ram's horn off the wall and blew into it. The blaring note left vibrations rolling through us. Should we be worried about being blown off the cliffs behind us? The others were looking warily around them, but I kept my eyes on the Grandis. I wasn't going to let fear stop me - not now, not ever.

A Dragon Rider stepped out from each alcove, their twisted silk scarves flapping from elbows and knees in the stiff breeze. Identical stony expressions painted each face. Words – too small for me to read from here - were burned on the leather strapping of their clothing. What would a Dragon Rider write on himself for safety or luck? Or were they tribute? Were they words to the heavens?

I didn't have time to dwell on them, as the Grandis blew the horn again - two sharp blasts and the Dragon Riders pulled out dark sticks from their belts. Or, at least, I thought they were sticks until fiery spurts burst from the ends and they cracked the whips sharply. Heads poked through the alcoves accompanied by roars and sulfurous smells. One wicked eye fixed me in its unblinking gaze. Orange and slit-pupiled, it looked like a window into hell. I felt a shiver begin at the base of my spine and ripple up through me, but with it came a giddy excitement. This is what I was here for.

The Grandis lowered the horn and called the first name. "High Castelan Savette Leedris."

The girl in the filmy sky silk stepped forward with a smirk for me. Of course. I called that one, didn't I? She glided down the line of snarling dragons as if she were selecting cloth for her next dress. A green one snapped his jaws at her, and although his head was larger than her entire body she did not flinch. She was courageous - I couldn't help but grudgingly approve of that.

She stopped in front of a shining crimson dragon, so sleek that his scales were barely raised. Lifting her chin, she looked at the Grandis and nodded. The Grandis flicked a wrist and the Dragon Rider whipped her dragon back into his alcove. Her name was written beside his: Eeamdor.

I felt a burst of envy mix with my excitement. What a fine dragon! Imagine being able to choose such an amazing creature to learn to ride - to live and die with?

The next one they called was another High Castelan - Daedru Tevish. He chose a gnarled golden dragon – Daacdid. Daacdid's lion mane and glittering black eyes flashed in the sun. I did not envy him his choice, although I liked the goals of the golden Dominion Color - the Goldens were diplomats. Where peace needed brokering, where disputes were irreconcilable, where boundaries were indefinite - that was where the golden Colors shone brightest. It was a far cry from red - the Color of war. Daedru and Savette would be opposed to one another from this moment on.

I was too nervous to remember the names of all those choosing dragons, but I did note that they chose dragons more for their color than anything else that I could determine. There seemed to be no preference for sleek over gnarled or aggressive over mild, but as the dragons' numbers thinned, the anxiety in those of us remaining intensified. When only three of us were left, the curly haired boy beside me chose the last black dragon with almost panicked haste. He must be desperate to be part of the Color of Towers - to build, defend and expand our sky cities. That didn't seem very exciting to me, but I would have gratefully taken that dragon, just as I'd gratefully take the red dragon two down from me who smelled so strongly that I thought my brain might melt out of my ears.

I was going to be last, just as I had known. It was hard to even see dragons from where we stood now. All the nearest had been claimed. There was only one more boy before me. He walked far down the line of alcoves and then back in the other direction, leaping back from one of the alcoves as the dragon within it snapped at him. He stumbled towards the edge of the precipice, scrambling back to solid land at the last moment before shakily pointing at an alcove I couldn't see. A cheer from the others who chose Green told me he would be an Explorer. I didn't know what I would be, but I was excited to be something.

There was a snicker from the group and when I glanced over it stopped. They were laughing at me - of course- but I couldn't tell who started it. I wanted to believe it was Savette, but that might just be because I didn't trust anyone who could afford sky silk.

The Grandis looked me in the eyes. "Amel Leafbrought."

I stepped forward, leaning on my crutch and trying for steady since I knew I couldn't manage graceful. I followed the line of alcoves, my pace slowed by my useless leg and the difficulty of finding a safe spot to place my stick with every step. To my relief, the Dragon Riders stared ahead in stony silence, not paying my awkward gait any more mind than they paid anyone else's pace.

I had yet to see a dragon in any of them, but I thought I could see one up ahead. A ruby head poked out from the alcove, roared and retreated in a gust of steam. In the next alcove, a white stole a glance at me before retreating again. Many whites had been claimed already. Wouldn't it be ironic if I were a Healer Color? Me, with the crippled leg?

A few alcoves down, a gnarled, flaky red peered at me with orange eyes. I swallowed hard. It would take nerves of steel to ride a dragon like that. Wouldn't it be just as strange for me to choose the red of war as the white of healing? What did I have to offer any of them? I was a leaf floating along the current, no choice on where it might take me or how fast, my only choice to ride the water and try not to sink.

Words and truth.

It was like a voice speaking right into my mind. Perhaps I really was crazy.

No, you're just listening to a dragon.

Wait. What? Did all the dragons talk like this? Why was I only hearing one?

Because we don't talk to humans if we don't have to.

Did this one *have* to talk to me for some reason? That didn't make sense. Who was I in the grand scheme of things? Nothing.

Today you won't be choosing a dragon.

I will choose one. I blinked back sudden tears. Even dragons didn't believe I should be here. I couldn't let this voice in my head rattle me. This was my only chance. I should choose quickly before the chance was ripped away like everything else. I reached for the white dragon. I could be a healer. Ironic or not, it was better than nothing.

Stop.

I froze.

You won't be choosing your dragon today because your dragon is choosing you.

A head poked out of an alcove at the far end of the line. I couldn't even make out what color it was as I hobbled forward.

Does it matter what color I am?

Not to me, it didn't.

Good.

I'd be whatever I needed to be. I was just grateful to get to try to live my dream - even if I failed. Some people don't even get to try.

We don't take to humans easily.

Dragons didn't take to humans? Then why have Dragon Riders at all?

By 'we' I meant Purple Dragons.

He said it just as I finally got close enough to make out his deep eggplant color just as his huge yellow eye winked at me. I gasped. He was gorgeous - sleek and lovely. I reached out a hand to touch him, but a leather gloved hand snatched mine away. The Dragon Rider stationed at the mouth of the alcove stared straight ahead as if I wasn't there, even though his hand gripped my wrist like a dog with a bone.

"He'll take your hand off. Don't touch."

"How do I choose him?"

The Dragon Rider looked me up and down. He was young for a rider- not many years older than I was – with a shining bald head and a stern expression that didn't match the youth and exuberance in his eyes.

"Pick a different dragon. Purple dragons – well, they're ornery and difficult. They have minds of their own. Even physically whole, I wouldn't bet on you living the week out on a Purple."

I swallowed. He'd noticed my limp. I bit the inside of my cheek. Stupid Amel, stupid. Of course, he noticed. It was the first thing anyone ever noticed about you. The only reason you're surprised is because you're so taken with the dragons that you thought you were like everyone else for a moment. You should remember that none of them respect you. They all think that you'll fail. You need to prove them wrong. I needed to start right here with this dragon.

I shook the gloved hand off my wrist, glared right in the Dragon Rider's eye and reached my hand further into the alcove. The yellow eye never blinked, but he didn't flame me or snap the arm off with a crunch of bone. Instead, he puffed a huff of steam and I bit back a curse as it left the skin of my arm red and tingling.

"I choose this dragon," I said, loudly enough for Grandis Dantriet to hear at the end of the line.

"He must like you," the Dragon Rider beside the alcove said. "That mild burn is like a love tap from him. Be careful. Next time he might melt the flesh right off the bone."

I sniffed and spun on my crutch, hobbling away.

Until we meet again.

A burst of excitement filled my chest. I wish I knew his name.

Raolcan.

I heard him say it at the same moment that I read it on the board as the Grandis finished chalking it next to my name. Somehow, I knew that name would change my life forever.

Chapter Two

WHEN I WAS SEVENTEEN months old, raiders invaded our village. My parents gathered up their children and ran to the forest, like everyone else. I don't remember that day, which is probably a good thing.

My grandfather was carrying me. I'm fifth of seven children and even though there were only six of us born then, my parents had their hands full. As we scrambled up the clay cliffs, my grandfather lost his footing and fell, dropping me and landing on top of me. He crushed my leg and hip.

Though it healed, it was never the same. I don't blame my grandfather. We were close until his death, but he always looked at me with a sad longing in his eyes. I think he could see me for what I could have been if the accident hadn't happened. But that's the thing – it did happen and pretending it didn't is foolish and it only holds me back. I won't let anything do that. I'm determined not to be any less than someone with two working legs.

If only people didn't all have to rub that crippled leg in my face as if it were a sin. That's the part that bothers me the most. I didn't do anything wrong – something wrong happened to me – so why does everyone act like I caused all this?

I hobbled down the long stone ledge with the rest of the recruits and I could hear them whispering about me. It's easy to hang back when you know you won't like what you hear. I couldn't help but listen as the conversation grew louder.

"Why is she even here? You know she won't be able to ride a dragon like that, much less train one."

"It's the rules, straw-for-brains. The Dragon Riders have to accept anyone who applies for the training. It's the code." That was the arrogant girl, Savette. She must be clever, too. Life worked that way. It gave some people everything and some people nothing, just to balance things out.

"Even if she dies the first day of training?"

"People always die. I just hope it weeds out the weak quickly. Dragon Riders need to be strong and focused. We don't need cripples or weaklings." That was the boy called Daedru. He'd chosen the color of diplomacy. Maybe he should rethink his choice. Not that he could now.

We were the Colors of our dragons whether we lived or died. There were no other choices for us. I knew that and it was why I was here. My parents loved me and they would house me and help me as long as I lived – I knew that – but I also saw how little we had and how much one mouth cost to feed, especially when that mouth couldn't do farm work. If I could have married, wifely chores would have been an option. Raising children and keeping house were hard work but didn't require as much brawn. But with my crushed hip, the wise women said I wouldn't bear children so that wasn't an option.

I would either live or die a Dragon Rider, now. We all would. No one left the service once they were recruited. You lived to serve as a Dragon Rider, or to serve Dragon Riders.

At least my family wouldn't starve trying to provide for me. I could be independent and earn my own keep – or die trying.

"How is she even going to get around here?"

I sighed a little at that because it was something I was worried about, too. Dragon School was nestled on the side of a massive butte. Alcoves built into the side of it served as the stables, dorms, banquet halls and the offices of the teachers and students. There were also housing sections for visiting Dragon Riders, an armory, and store rooms. Each of them was connected by long narrow outer ledges and spiraling steps or ladders going up and down between levels. Climbing the ladders to the stables on the very top level had taken all my strength this morning and I was already lagging behind the rest of the students. Just going from one place to the next was going to take all my stamina. At least I'd be in great shape.

"Hey, girl," one of them called back to me. "Dinner starts at four bells. If you don't get there in time I'm taking your portion."

He could take all the food he could find and he still wouldn't take my dream away. A little hunger was nothing new for me. It took some effort to descend the ladders to the third level. Levels at Dragon School were numbered from the top down so that level three was three levels below the stables.

By the time I reached the dining hall, the meal was well underway. Long tables covered with white cloth were heaped with food. The smell of salmon with lemon sauce was mouthwatering. The tables close to the wide open windows were raised on daises and were clearly for senior Dragon Riders and instructors. I saw Grandis Dantriet eating at one of them. He was the only instructor I'd met so far. He'd met us on the boat this morning before we were ferried to the base of the mountain.

"New recruits?" he'd asked gruffly. At our nods, he'd continued, "By leaving on this raft you signify that you accept your recruitment into the Dragon Riders. No recruit will be denied, but every year many recruits die and those who cannot gentle a dragon will leave the recruitment program and become servants of the Dragon Riders. There is no leaving this life with us other than death, be ye noble or common, great or small, sick or well. Do all accept this?"

We'd chorused a 'yes' as he signaled to the ferry man to pull us across the river. From the ferry, we'd gone straight up to the stables. It was strange to realize he was just one man among others, not a great golden god who we must bow before. Even knowing it wasn't enough to shake my awe away.

At the table furthest from the windows, back in a dull corner, were the recruits I'd arrived with. They sat in a line on benches and ate quietly. I took a seat on the end of the bench. No one looked at me, but I didn't care. There was salmon still available and I hadn't had more than a few scraps of bread in the past week while I'd been traveling. I'd hitched rides from town to town on farmer's wagons or tradesman's carts – anyone who was willing to take a passenger along the way. They didn't charge anything – except conversation – and it was safer than walking where thieves or troublemakers could cause a lone traveler harm.

"Why can't we sit with them?" A dark-haired, good-looking boy pointed to the table beside ours. All the people at that table were young, too, but they all wore gray leather clothing that fit snugly over their bodies and were cinched tight with buckles at waist, elbows, knees and practically everywhere else. They looked almost like Dragon Riders, except they wore no braids or flowing silk scarves, and the full Dragon Riders wore black leather.

Savette rolled her eyes. I was beginning to find her show of arrogance entertaining. At least she was true to form - a font of information.

"They're Inducted. They're a step above us. When we gentle our dragons so they can be ridden, then we'll be inducted into the Dragon Riders and that will be us."

His smile bordered on a smirk when he addressed her again. Was he being flirtatious? "And what about them?"

He pointed at another long table. These people were slightly older and wore brown leathers with one or two silken scarves. Some wore a braid in their hair, others didn't. I was glad that he was asking. Unlike others here, my childhood had focused more on how to grind grain into flour and properly oil the plow straps than it had on the inner-workings of Dragon School.

"Those are Sworn. They've moved to the next level of training and they've sworn their loyalty at court. Some of them get to go out in the field and be trained individually by full Dragon Riders. I swear, Jael, did your tutors teach you nothing?"

"They didn't have your melodious voice, Savette."

She scoffed, but the way her cheeks pinked she was clearly enjoying herself.

"And what about the tables with the colors?" I asked, so caught up in the explanation that I forgot myself.

The table went silent and the people closest to me looked away. Savette focused on her food like she was going to write an exam on the contents of her plate. The good looking one – Jael - spoke after long minutes of silence.

"Look, don't take it personally, but none of us wants to get too attached to you. We know that you'll die in the first couple of lessons and ... well, the thing is ... well ..." His eyes were full of pity as he stumbled on his words.

"What he means to say is that we don't want to have to feel bad when you die. You shouldn't have come here in the first place," Savette said, harshly.

I bit into my bread and blinked back wetness in my eyes. Their words stung. And they weren't true. I wouldn't die in the first week. I'd show them all. They'd see that they were wrong about me and then I'd find some way to show them that I didn't need their pity any more than I needed their help.

"They're Colors," the girl to one side of me said. Her eyes were a shocking blue. The words burst out of her like she'd been holding them in with her breath. "That's why their silken scarves are all one color at each table. They aren't full Dragon Riders yet, but they will be really soon. They've been approved by their Color and all they have to do is pass the final test."

She looked away quickly like she was afraid to catch my limp. I wanted to snap at her, but she was the only one who'd answered at all. Perhaps I shouldn't say no to friendliness, no matter how tiny a sliver of it was offered. I ducked my head in thanks and kept my mouth buttoned so I could watch the room. If I was on my own, I'd need to learn as much as I could, and that meant watching everything all the time.

It was a good thing I was watching, or I wouldn't have seen Grandis Dantriet look up from his salmon, his sharp gaze cutting through the room to me. When he met my gaze, he didn't look away like everyone else. He held it for three breaths, looking for something – I was sure – and then, finally, looking away. Whatever he was looking for, he seemed satisfied and I swallowed down my nerves and ate my own food. He hadn't sent me away when he saw my limp. Maybe he knew something no one else did – no one except for me.

Chapter Three

I WOKE WITH A START and almost fell out of the upper bunk I was in. By the time I'd gotten to it the night before, everyone in the girls' dorm had claimed the bottom ones. The redhead who was sleeping beneath me had turned her back coldly when I asked if she'd consider switching and I hadn't had the energy to ask anyone else and deal with extra rejection. I rubbed my eyes, gathered my things and made my way slowly down the ladder. I could work ladders, it was just more difficult because I had to hop down every step, holding the rung carefully with two hands and dragging my bad leg.

If it wasn't for the fact that no one here thought I would last the week out, I'd love the girls' dorm. The bunks were solidly built and soft with white, crisp sheets, and woolen blankets piled high on every one. I'd never slept so well. The ceiling was high- vaulted with huge windows lining one stone wall, open to the outdoors. Silken curtains floated in the breeze before them. I was beginning to understand that Dragon Riders were outdoors people. They lived, breathed, bled and died in the outdoors. I'd never been very outdoorsy. It was hard to get very far over uneven ground on my crutch and most of the chores

I could help my family with were done inside, things that required quick hands rather than a strong back.

I found the fresh, breezy dorms stimulating. Fortunately, I was the first up, so I had time to wash at the long stone basin the washroom at the back of the dorm. Someone had carved a bathroom area out and water splashed into the long wash basin in a continuous flow. There was even a large area at the back where it dripped down from the roof as if it were constantly raining. If I had more time I'd like to see what it felt like to wash under that rain, but for now, the flow in the basin would be enough. I'd never expected to live in luxury like this, with hot meals and water delivered right to the washroom. If I really did die this week, it would only be after living in a virtual wonderland.

I tied my waist-length dark hair back and scrubbed my face clean. I didn't have to be pretty today, I had to be functional and that meant no hair getting in the way of the work. I tucked my plain shirt into the rope belt, trying to make it as streamlined as the clothing of the Inducted I'd seen the night before. We hadn't been issued Dragon Rider clothing yet, so I'd have to make do with my peasant clothes and hope I could get them tight enough not to interfere with the work.

"You won't be able to make them any better no matter how hard you try," Savette said, walking to the basin beside me and splashing her perfect, high cheekbones with water so that they pinked up like a summer rose. "Peasant clothes will never look like Dragon Rider clothes."

She wore soft green wool that hugged her form almost as well as Dragon Rider leathers, and small woolen ties imitated what I'd seen in the dining hall. I didn't usually envy wealth –

what point would there be in that? I may as well envy her beauty – but I did envy the functionality of those clothes. It would be nice to be able to be prepared for what was coming.

"Breakfast starts next bell, but if I were you I'd get a move on. We only have a half-bell to eat and if we are late to the stables there will be penalties." Her face was impassive but I saw a flicker of something in her eyes.

"Don't warn her," the redhead complained, coming into the washroom and quickly stripping out of her silken nightdress to step under the showering rain. Her voice was muffled by the water. "If she gets cut first it gives us a better chance!"

I didn't look at Savette as I left the washroom but as I walked by I whispered, "Thank you."

She hadn't needed to warn me, and yet she did. Why? I had plenty of time to puzzle about it as I left the dorms and began to climb the ladders to the first level – the stables. The rock of Dragon School glinted brightly with flecks of mica under the sun of the cloudless sky. I was enjoying myself despite the difficulty of the climb. I slung my crutch through the back of my belt and took the rungs of the ladders one at a time.

By the time I reached the second level, the bell for breakfast had rung. I took a moment to catch my breath, looking out over the rolling hills and river delta below the cliffs. Somewhere out there, my family was beginning the work of the day. I could almost see my mother's smile in my mind's eye. A pang of homesickness tugged at me but I swallowed it down, blinking back tears. They would be fine – better off, even – without me. I needed to remember that my decision was the best thing for all of them. Besides, it was too late to change my mind now. I belonged to Dragon School now.

A rushing sound filled the air and I hastily brushed my sleeve across my eyes in time to look up and see the belly of a purple dragon rear up in front of me. Its massive wings blocked out the sun and a keening sound filled the air. I froze, fear and fascination warring within me. What would it be like to ride on the back of such a magnificent beast? This wasn't Raolcan, was it?

Not a chance, little human.

It spoke to me, too! Would I be able to hear all dragons now? There was a snickering sound in my mind, and then the dragon's belly raced past, the scales blurring in the speed of its passing, and it was racing – up, up, up – until it was nothing but a black silhouette between me and the sun. I gasped and let myself enjoy the wonder of the moment. I lived in a school where dragons were as every-day as water. What could be more amazing than that? A single "bing" – a half bell – rang and I scrambled back onto the ladder. I had two more levels to climb on the face of this cliff or there would be consequences.

Now that I'd seen a dragon in flight - so close that I could hear its thoughts and then so far that it was nothing but a speck in the sky - now that I'd felt the rush of its wings and seen the power of its bunched muscles unleashed into flight, now I couldn't think of not trying to ride one. A sudden image filled my mind – me falling through the air towards the sharp rocks below. I squashed it down and brought up a better mental image – me soaring on the back of a dragon, free and liberated as the dragon himself. I clung to that thought as I climbed higher. Whatever happened from here on in had to include that. It just had to.

Chapter Four

AS I ARRIVED AT LEVEL One, the purple dragon returned in a spectacular soaring dive. It caught the edge of the cliffs with outstretched talons and hung there for a moment. Its rider leapt off, landing solidly on the rim of the cliff – just inches from the edge. The dragon turned his head to the rider as if he were speaking and then ducked low and crept into one of the alcoves. What kept them there? Did they stay of their own accord? Was Raolcan there somewhere? I wanted to see him again. Maybe he would have some ideas for me about how to stay alive. The Dragon Rider gave me a mock salute and then ducked into the alcove after his dragon.

"Amel Leafbrought?" I spun at the sound of Grandis Dantriet's voice. He smiled. "You must be very eager to be here before the bell has sounded."

"I didn't want to be late, sir."

He looked at me for a long moment, his eyes trailing to my back where my crutch was still fastened. Blushing, I pulled it off my back and secured it under my arm.

"Good thinking," he said at last. "The first class of the day is Tack and Stables. Your instructor is Anda Elfar."

I nodded and followed his gaze to an alcove down the ledge. Red curtains swirled outside the door and leather tack hung from more hooks, pegs, and rails than I'd ever seen in one place. I made my way to the alcove and peered inside to see long wooden benches and tables polished to a gleam. They faced a raised dais with various maps pinned up behind it. I took a seat at the nearest bench, hoping I'd chosen correctly.

After a moment, a short, muscled woman with cropped gray hair and a pleasant but weathered face came in and strode to the front of the room. She acknowledged me with a nod but seemed caught up in her own thoughts. Voices from outside the door were soon followed by a wave of other Dragon Rider hopefuls. I recognized Savette and Daedru as well as the dark-haired boy from last night who pitied me, and the red-haired girl who slept below me and definitely did NOT pity me. Judging by their bubbling chatter, most of them were well on their way to becoming friends. I focused on the instructor, waiting for the lesson to begin. I might not be the social princess of our group, but I was here to learn.

"Your first work every morning will be with Tack and Stables. This is the only lesson in my class that will involve any sitting down," Grandis Anda Elfar's voice cut through any noise like an axe. "Come to class in the morning prepared to work. Servants clean and cook for us. We clean and feed the dragons. Servants will clean your clothes. We oil and mend the tack for the dragons. See yourself as a servant and the work will be easy. See yourself as above it and you won't last the week."

"You'd send us to the servant halls for being bad at Tack?" a golden-haired boy asked.

The Grandis lifted an eyebrow and crossed her arms. "Name?"

"Dannil Evermore."

"When I began here I was like all of you – foolish and hopeful. A boy named Javen Taydon began in the same wave as I did. He was of high rank and blood." Anda paused, looking out the massive open windows at the roiling clouds on the horizon. Was she seeing the boy from her past in her mind's eye? "He was not attentive to his tack. A week into our training he slipped and the mid-strap meant to secure him caught him as he fell – only the stitching holding the buckle was worn. It snapped and he fell to his death. Every time I repair a mid-strap buckle I remember how long he screamed before he hit the ground." Our silence was filled with horror. "If you fail at Tack and Stables you will not be a servant. You will be dead."

I swallowed, imagining a boy falling, falling, falling to his death simply because he forgot to check the stitching on a strap. I'd have to take Tack very seriously.

As Grandis Elfar launched into a lecture on oils and stitching, the feeling that I was being watched crept over me. I tried to focus harder. Knowing the correct oils to use and what to look for in our tack was a life or death matter. I couldn't afford to be distracted. The feeling remained.

"The tack in front of you is the tack assigned to your dragon. Every morning when you clean your dragon's stall you will inspect and clean your tack." The Grandis seemed unaffected by whatever was bothering me, her lesson rolling off her tongue like she'd said it a thousand times before – maybe she had.

I glanced over my shoulder and saw a Dragon Rider leaning against the frame of our class window, his bald head cocked to the side. He appeared to be studying me. Purple silk scarves of varying prints fluttered at his neck, elbows and knees and waist. I frowned. Was that the Dragon Rider who had grabbed my hand when I reached for Raolcan? I thought it might be. Somehow, I'd caught his attention and that couldn't be a good thing.

He was at least five years older than I was, judging by his looks, and his face and head were dark from sun, his unshaven scruff black. I couldn't tell from his expression if he was judging me or merely curious. Either way, I fought down a shiver. What could he want?

I redoubled my focus on Grandis Elfar. She was explaining what use different stitching was in the proper function of our tack.

"You will care for your own tack and no one else's unless asked. Every morning your first tasks will be to care for your tack, muck out your dragon's stall and carry his water. Failure at any of these tasks will spell disaster. These are not only chores, they are life-giving work. Do not forget that in Dragon School the smallest of tasks is important. Your attention to detail and focus on the little things will determine your ability to do greater things. No one succeeds as a Dragon Rider if they do not attend their tack and stable."

The red-haired girl from earlier raised a hand and Grandis Elfar nodded to her. "When we are full Dragon Riders and we have the responsibilities of executing the Dominion good, will others care for our dragons?"

I glanced at the window, but the Dragon Rider was gone. I felt strangely disappointed, even though I'd been trying to appear like I didn't care what he was interested in. Maybe I'd see him here again.

Grandis Elfar looked at a list on the wall before responding, "High Castelan Starie Atrelan?"

"Yes," the girl agreed.

"Your dragon's health will always be your own responsibility. Today, to reinforce the need to care for your dragon, you will muck out both his stall and my dragon's stall – under my supervision. I, like all Dragon Riders, would never leave such an important task to someone else without supervising it myself."

Starie groaned and I heard a snicker from behind me. Grandis Elfar's face turned dark.

"You think this is a laughing matter? Your name?"

It was the good-looking dark-haired boy. "Castelan Jael Woelran."

"We don't usually muck stalls on the first day, Jael, but it looks like this class will be doing it. They can thank you for the privilege. We'll talk more about tack tomorrow. Today, we muck stalls. Form a line at the door."

I hobbled over to where the line was forming and found my place right behind Starie. She looked back at me, grimaced and then sniffed and turned away. What had I ever done to her?

"There's a hidden pulley system for the buckets," a voice whispered in my ear.

I turned around to see Savette looking up at the ceiling, an indifferent look on her face. For someone who pretended not to care about me, she sure seemed to be going out of her way to help. I tried to catch her eye to thank her, but Grandis Elfar was already calling us to order.

We followed her brisk pace down the long line of Dragon alcoves. The name of each dragon was carved into the rock above his head. How old and permanent must they be to have someone carve their name in the rock?

The alcoves of the dragons nearest to us were lush and smelled of sweet hay and something nutty. Warm air drifted from them and I thought I saw the glow of braziers within.

"These are Dragon Rider mounts," Grandis Elfar said as we walked. "They are to be honored and respected. Allies, not servants."

After long minutes, we turned a corner to a new line of stables along the curve of the ridge.

"These are the mounts of visiting Dragon Riders." The Grandis called back her explanations in a loud clear voice. I wondered if it was trained to be heard by others in the air. Would it be noisy to fly on the back of a Dragon with air rushing past you from the speed?

These alcoves seemed more uniform and no names or special decorations were present, but they were clean and fresh. They seemed to go on and on to the point where my crutch was irritating my arm pit. I was going to have to get used to this walk. My speed was flagging and the Dannil Evermore pushed past me with three other boys.

"These are the dragons of the Sworn and Inducted. Watch yourself here and do not go to close to the openings. These dragons are not fully trained."

The stables here were alive with activity. Sworn and Inducted busily cleaned alcoves and hauled water, calling and laughing together. I watched with a hint of longing. They looked like families or very close friends. And they seemed to enjoy their life here as trainees. Perhaps there was a life here for me, if I could find my bearings and make friends.

I glanced behind me. Savette was the only one who hadn't pushed past me, but I couldn't catch her eye. She was focused on watching those who ranked above us. Knowing her, she was probably memorizing every detail of their work to lecture us about later. What made a high-born lady in pretty clothes so keen on understanding how things worked? It was an admirable trait to have. If only Savette wasn't so cold, perhaps we could be friends.

"Don't fall behind!" Grandis Elfar's voice cut through my thoughts and I took a deep breath and picked up my pace. I was already winded, but I didn't dare to show that I couldn't keep up. "We have now reached the area of recently caught dragons. Watch your step with caution and follow the orders of the Green Dragon Riders. Recently caught or hatched dragons are in their care."

Here, Dragon Riders with green silk scarves guarded alcoves or worked busily around the alcoves. I couldn't tell what they were doing, but the work seemed focused and intent.

"Wild Dragons that are caught and then gentled here by a rider form a bond with only that rider for life. The ones raised in captivity lack the spirit and individuality of wild dragons," Savette said, as if to herself.

So, that was why they had fresh recruits choose and care for a dragon. We had the opportunity to bond with our dragons. It was a very dangerous way to do things. And what kept them contained in their alcoves?

"See the Dragon Riders standing between alcoves? They are maintaining the ward that keeps freshly caught Dragons in their alcoves. Loyal Dragons don't need to be contained, but Mustang Dragons – wild ones – need to be gentled first." Savette was still pretending she wasn't talking to me. Should I ask her a question or go along with her acting? I decided to ask. I needed to be sure I hadn't heard her wrong.

"Are the Green Dragon Riders going to gentle them?"

She laughed. "No, Amel. We are. Our first job as trainees is to gentle a dragon and take the First Flight. If we live through that first flight, we will have passed the first test and we'll be considered Initiates of Dragon School."

Her words were punctuated by the crack of a whip. One of the Green Dragon Riders had cracked his whip to contain a snorting white dragon.

I swallowed. We had to ride a wild dragon to be considered full initiates? No wonder everyone kept thinking I wouldn't last the week out. If I thought managing narrow rock walkways and ladders with a crutch was bad, how was I going to ride a wild dragon – even Raolcan who seemed to like me? I was going to need all my courage.

I wouldn't have chosen a girl without courage.

I smiled at his words in my head. I wasn't alone in this, was I? I had an ally.

Chapter Five

RAOLCAN? HE MUST BE close! I could hardly hold myself back from rushing to his alcove, but Grandis Elfar was giving instructions.

"Your dragons are not yet tame or bonded to you. Do not try to touch them. The Green Dragon Riders at each pen will strengthen the wards to keep the dragon on one side of the pen while you clean. Shovel any refuse into the grated area at the back of the pen and it will fall into the pits. Then, flush the alcoves with water and lay out fresh straw. Fill the trough with drinking water and the tray with feed. If you have problems, call for help. I'm not here to look beautiful. I'm here to teach you to care for your dragon. Is that understood?"

We nodded together and the Grandis marched us down the line of alcoves, nodding to each of us as we found our alcove. The dragons weren't organized by color like they were in the other areas. I kept walking and walking, wondering why Raolcan always seemed to be at the end of the line. Savette's red dragon was long before Raolcan and she entered his alcove with her usual grace, leaving me alone with Grandis Elfar.

"This is your dragon?" she asked, when we finally reached his alcove at the very end of the line.

It was quiet here, far from the bustle of the rest of the Stables. I could hear birds screeching in the sky and see the ocean far out on the horizon. It must be hard to be caged here so close to freedom when he was used to going wherever he pleased.

You have no idea how hard it is.

"Yes." I didn't even have to look. His mental voice was becoming familiar to me.

"You chose a purple. They are very rare." Her mouth thinned as she pressed her lips together firmly and her eyes grew hard. "A purple is a treasure to all of us. Treat him with extreme care."

Her expression was confusing – judgmental and condemning as if I'd committed a crime.

"Why are you so angry?" I asked.

She shook her head and tsked. "Just treat him well."

She was stalking away before I could say anything else, leaving me red-cheeked and embarrassed. What did I do to make her so angry?

You chose me. Or, at least, she thinks you did. She doesn't realize that purple dragons always choose for themselves. She's Black. Towers are about stability.

That was it? She was angry that I chose Purple? Had she wanted me to choose Black like her?

No, she's afraid you will waste me and she thinks I'm a valuable resource. If you fail to ride me, no one else will be able to. They'll lose me as a resource.

I entered Raolcan's alcove and saw he was leaning against one wall, leaving most of the alcove clear. A shovel and pitchfork hung at the back of the alcove. I leaned my crutch carefully against the wall and took the shovel down. I'd have to work carefully to clear the stall with one hand on the shovel and one using my crutch. I concentrated, lining the shovel up so I could slide it along the ground and plow any refuse to the back where the grate leading to the pits was.

I worked silently, allowing myself to get lost in the difficulty of the unfamiliar task.

It will get easier as you adjust.

Did he choose me because he wanted to be free again and he thought that I was the least likely of my wave of trainees to succeed?

That's an unfair thought. You don't trust easily, do you?

It was going to be tough to be friends with someone who could read my thoughts. I had plenty of nice ones, but it's not easy to grow up with extra challenges and fewer opportunities and not grow a little bitter.

So, you don't trust easily and you doubt everyone's motives. We have that in common. I don't trust humans.

If he didn't choose me because he thought I was weak, then why did he choose me? What did I have to offer?

If you want to ask me, then ask. Address me like an equal.

I'm sorry. I don't mean to belittle you. I'm just not used to this. Help me not to be unfair to you. Why did you choose me?

I hoped you'd be able to understand me. Neither of us trusts easily. Neither of us likes people very much. Both of us are captives – you to a leg that holds you back. Me by bonds of magic that have imprisoned me and kept me here. And neither of us has a chance to escape. I thought that perhaps we could understand each other – help each other. Was I wrong?

I was done scraping the floor. I hung the shovel up and went to work with the bucket. The same water that flowed in the dorms trickled over a rock ledge here. A spout had been set up to catch the flowing water and direct it in an accessible stream. I filled the bucket, carefully hobbling to the mouth of the alcove and letting it wash across the floor.

Was he wrong about me? Could I help anyone else? I wanted to think that I was a good person with a kind heart. I did feel bad that he was caged here when he should be free to fly.

That's a start.

But his imprisonment was my opportunity. I didn't feel nearly bad enough about his situation because I knew that it made opportunity possible for me.

At least you know that. You can acknowledge your selfish attitude about this.

Do you want me to pour any water over you? I would want a bath if I was trapped in this alcove.

He shivered. Was that mental laughter I was hearing?

I couldn't imagine anything more horrible than purposely pouring buckets of water over myself. You humans are very strange.

I hung the bucket back up and laid out fragrant hay from where it was stored. Why didn't Raolcan get a fancy brazier?

Because I'm not gentled yet. Not broken to their ways.

I finished up and walked to stand in front of him, glancing over my shoulder at the guard by the door. He wasn't watching but I didn't want to risk getting in trouble for this.

What do you want, Raolcan? Your freedom?

That's gone forever now, girl.

I'm Amel. Amel Leafbrought. If you can't have your freedom, then what do you want?

A purpose.

Just like me.

And a friend.

I reached a hand out - slowly and gently. There was a glint of violence in his eye and he snapped his jaw. I pulled the hand back, instinctually but then reached out again. I had to be courageous. I couldn't be a friend if I expected him to be the one to always reach out to me. Carefully, I let my hand extend - inch by inch - towards his snout. I kept my gaze locked on his serpentine eye, careful not to even breathe aggressively. I laid my hand gently on his snout, feather-light.

I'll be your friend. I swallowed hard. I could feel my heart beating as fast as a dragon could fly.

Not quite as fast.

I drew my hand back slowly and smiled. So, I had a friend. That was unexpected.

A dragon friend can be dangerous.

Maybe he should have led with that.

Chapter Six

I TURNED AT A SCUFFLING sound in the doorway. The young Dragon Rider I'd seen leap off his purple dragon was frozen in the alcove entrance, hands held up and a look of horror on his face. I frowned. Was he hurt somehow?

"Don't move," he whispered.

I froze. What did he see? A deadly spider? A snake? I tried to look without turning my head, but it was hard to see anything in that position. How could I know if the danger was growing closer if I stayed totally still? And couldn't Raolcan deal with spiders and snakes if they came in his alcove?

I certainly can.

"Don't even breathe."

Well, that sounded like bad advice. I went ahead and ignored it.

"Back up slowly to where I am."

I leaned into my crutch and slowly slid one foot after another backward to where he was.

"What is it?" I whispered, wide-eyed.

We were inches from each other, and he breathed a trembling sigh of relief. His dark face was washed out and his hand trembled on the doorframe of the alcove.

"You shouldn't touch an un-gentled dragon." His voice was burred and raspy, like he was holding back emotion.

"It's alright. I was just getting to know him." I tried to smile, but his attitude was frightening. Why was he so worried about Raolcan? Should I be?

I won't harm you. Intentionally.

He ran a palm over his face and looked at me with a firm expression, like he was trying to be patient or controlling his temper. Long minutes of silence hung between us before he spoke again. I felt a little uncomfortable at the attention. People didn't usually look at my face. They usually looked at my leg and then looked away quickly. I felt like I might blush from the attention. I tried not to look away. Other girls wouldn't, would they? They would find that kind of attention perfectly normal. I didn't want to be different than anyone else would be.

"Let's walk you back to your classroom. You're taking Tack and Stables this morning, right? Your wave arrived yesterday?"

It seemed like he was trying to be kind and I didn't want to disappoint him. I nodded shyly. He glanced at the chalkboard beside the alcove where my name was written next to Raolcan's.

"And you chose Raolcan? A purple?"

"Yes."

"Purple is a fine choice." He placed his hand gently on the small of my back, steering me towards the entrance of the alcove. I didn't really want to go but I didn't want to cause a scene, either. After all, I'd be back here tomorrow cleaning out Raolcan's alcove again.

Goodbye, Raolcan. Hopefully, he didn't take it personally.

I'm used to people not trusting me. It's only fair. I don't trust them.

I hoped he'd eventually trust me.

Trust is a precious gift. You've given me yours. You can believe it will be reciprocated.

He was very wise.

For a dragon?

Was that a mental laugh?

"I didn't choose him," I told the Dragon Rider. "He chose me."

He gave me a hesitant look but it turned to a smile as we left the alcove and slowly walked down the long ledge. He kept pace with me, even though I was a lot slower than he was.

"If you make it through your First Flight you'll be a Purple in training." He seemed pleased about that. "We value courage, but we also value people who use their heads."

"We?"

He flicked the scarf slung low around his waist. A matching one ringed his neck, both a deep purple that looked good against his dark skin and eyes. Light glinted off his scalp. Did he shave it? What would I look like if I shaved my head? Hopefully, I'd never know.

"My Color is Purple, just as yours will be if you become a full initiate. There aren't many of us." His conversation was easy mannered, as was his pace. I enjoyed falling into a rhythm with him. He carried calm with him, like a permanent pack on his back.

"Why aren't there many Purples?"

He shrugged. "We catch very few Purple dragons. They're reclusive. They fly their own paths through the clouds, not like other dragons that form flocks or migrate together."

So, Raolcan was like me in that. Reclusive. A loner. I liked him more as I got to know him.

As we drew closer to where the other trainees were working I found it harder to pay attention to his easy conversation. What was going on over there? The trainee alcoves looked like an anthill had been turned over. Trainees I didn't know bustled in and out of alcoves with hurried speed, their hair and garments rumpled and dirty. I saw Savette outside of hers, tucking a loose strand of hair behind her ear as she bandaged another girl's hand. Two more trainees sat on the ledge, nursing injuries, their clothing singed and dirty.

"What happened to them?" I was aghast.

The Purple Dragon Rider looked surprised at my question. "They're cleaning their dragon's alcoves. Un-gentled dragons are dangerous but if trainees can't learn to dodge a stream of fire and shake off a few burns they won't be able to handle the next part of the gentling process. Besides, being near their dragons is the first step towards helping them bond with their dragons. The dragons need to get to know their scents, no matter how dangerous the process might be."

"The Grandis didn't mention any of that." I couldn't keep the horror out of my words. They should have been warned. They could be seriously injured if their dragons acted like that! I couldn't help but feel a bit guilty – my experience with Raolcan had been entirely different.

Brutes.

He must still be picking up my thoughts, though I didn't know if he meant the other dragons or my fellow trainees.

Both.

"They're dragons. What did you expect?" The Dragon Rider's tone was neutral, like he was curious more than anything.

I blushed but said nothing. Should I admit that Raolcan was speaking in my mind? Wouldn't I sound insane? What if they reassigned me to a new dragon? I didn't want that. I was beginning to like the deep purple dragon. His brow was furrowed, like I was a puzzle to be figured out.

"What's your name, trainee?"

"Amel Leafbrought."

"I think it's likely we'll meet again. Work hard, Amel Leafbrought. We accept only the best in Purple."

I nodded and he started to leave, but I called after him, surprised at my own boldness. "What is your name, Dragon Rider?"

"Leng Shardson." His eyes twinkled as he answered, but his expression remained serious. I wanted him to know that I was worthy of Purple, but I wasn't sure how to do that. And what if I couldn't convince him? What if I said the wrong thing and looked stupid?

I watched him stride away, watched his slightly bow-legged walk and his careful movements, like he was always balancing on the back of a dragon. Did he shave his head to make it easier to fly without hair swirling around his face? I should consider what to do with my own hair. Savette probably had ideas about that.

My pace was slow as I worked my way past the alcoves. I found it frustrating, even though I was used to it. At home, I hadn't had to walk far, but the stables alone were as large as my village and the five others in our area combined. I'd never had to walk so far before and being slow chafed. At least it gave me time to take in all the details.

Insignia were draped on some dragon doors. I assumed these ones belonged to Castelans or High Castelans, because Savette's alcove had an intricately designed banner hanging over her door. Castelans ran the Towers of the Dominion. And Towers governed the towns and villages surrounding them. High Castelans lorded over groups of Towers. Until I'd arrived here, I'd never seen a tower in my life, and now I was living in the most majestic of all the towers – Dragon School. Not that it was man-made. It was carved from the great land divide – a natural up-thrust of layered rock and waterfalls. Tufts of mist rose up from the wet river delta below as the golden sun burned across the land. The river flashed, snake-like between greens and browns of shrubbery until it boiled brown and churning into the silver ocean. I allowed myself to be distracted by it for a moment.

A scream shredded the air and as I turned to see where it was coming from, someone ran past me, knocking my crutch out. I stumbled, falling onto the ledge and grazing my knee. Ouch. I tried to stand, but a second person crashed into me, knocking me flat on my face. My chin hit the rock. Defensively, I curled into a ball, wrapping my arms around my head. Foot-steps and yells were all around me and I felt my heart beating at a dizzying speed. I needed to get up so that I wasn't kicked.

I scrambled up, recovering my crutch. The rush of people was past me, but someone was still screaming, and cries filled the air. I hobbled forward. At the end of the row of recruit dragon alcoves, the rest of the students were clustered. Someone was rushing from the other side of the stables with a stretcher under one arm.

"Back up! Back up!" That was Grandis Elfar yelling. She and the man with the stretcher shoved their way through the knot of people. By the time I made it to the edge of the group, Savette was pushing her way out of the knot, face white and mouth wide in distress.

"Savette?" I laid a hand on her trembling arm. "Are you hurt?"

"No," she gasped. Her eyes flicked wildly until they settled on something behind me. I turned to see she was staring at her dragon's alcove.

"Is your dragon alright?"

"What?" She was in shock.

"Your dragon - Eeamdor – is he alright?"

She looked at me like I'd grown another head. "Who cares about dragons? It's Dannil. He... he..."

Her voice trailed off and then a surge of the crowd came towards us. I held on to her to avoid being swept away. As the other trainees moved behind us I finally had a look at the center of the group. Dannil lay in a pool of blood, while a dragon school medic tried to bind his wound. The screaming had stopped. He was unconscious on the stretcher they'd brought – and he was missing his right arm.

I swallowed back a sudden wave of nausea. His dragon had bit off his arm?

"How -?"

"They're dragons, Amel," Savette said. Her expression was severe. "They aren't pets."

The medics strapped him to the stretcher and Grandis Elfar finished rigging a rope to a pulley against the rock face. They were going to lower him down to another level of dragon school. I'd been wondering what they did when people couldn't climb the ladders and now I knew.

What would happen to Dannil? Would he come back and try to ride his dragon once he was healed? I didn't realize I'd said that out loud until Savette scoffed.

"He lost his right arm. You have to be strong and healthy to ride a dragon and no one can do it with a missing limb."

I let go of her like I'd been burned by the touch. Anger and frustration clouded my mind so that all my thoughts were in shards and spiky shattered pieces that wanted nothing but to harm and damage. I clamped down tightly on the impulse and tried to smooth my face and make my breathing easy. Anger and frustration did nothing to erase an insult.

"That's enough for today. We're breaking early for noonday meal. You'll be given further instructions after your meal," Grandis Elfar's voice cut across the ambient noise and we all fell silent. "Let today be a lesson to you. Tack and Stables is not a game or a job for servants. The wild dragon that has been brought here for you to gentle is not a pet or a pony. You must have your wits about you during even the simplest of tasks or you will end up like your friend – maimed for life. Dismissed."

I followed the line of people to the ladders heading down to the dining hall level, but my eyes wandered to the hidden pulley. Things around here sure would go quicker for me if I could use those to ascend and descend levels. I felt a lurch in my stomach at the thought of swaying out over that deadly drop, but I needed to find an edge. Any edge. Savette's expression as she spoke about Dannil was enough to convince me that I needed to change people's minds about me, or they'd always be thinking of me as "that crippled girl" instead of a Dragon Rider.

Chapter Seven

"NO ONE LIKES TO SIT inside when the weather is beautiful, not even instructors." Grandis Leman was our instructor after lunch. His lips had a bitter quirk to them and the classroom smelled musty and neglected. Perhaps he was serious about spending all his time out of doors. "This is Maps, Geography, and Regions. It's better to learn these skills practically from the backs of your dragons, but until your First Flight there are only books to help you."

Grandis Leman talked with the bored air of someone who would rather be anywhere else. His nose was like a wide blade, so dominant that it was almost all I noticed – even before his age or hair color. He'd wrapped his hair back in a silken bandana, though it flowed down almost as long as my own and was interspersed with braids. Maybe that was what I should do with mine.

"You'll see three textbooks in front of you. Do all of you know how to read?"

By Dominion decree, every child was schooled from the ages of five to ten. There should be no one who was illiterate. Though literacy and numeracy weren't all that helpful in a peasant's life of farming, it made things easier if peasants were recruited to the military, taken as servants of Castelans, or volunteered as Dragon Riders. Most serving jobs required basic literacy.

"Excellent," Grandis Leman said, his tone belying his words. "There are three books in front of you: *Maps of the Dominion*, *Lantris' Cartography*, and *Jogler's Kingdoms, Regions, and Unknown Lands*. These are precious and belong to Dragon School. Treat them with care. You will read them all thoroughly before the week is over and you will be tested on them after your First Flight. The test is standard. Failure is unacceptable."

Daedru's hand shot up and Grandis Leman waved to him. "What happens if we fail?"

"Don't." Grandis Leman punctuated his reply with the flat of his hand slamming on the tabletop beside him. I wouldn't be asking him any questions. "I dislike being cooped up indoors, as I trust is true of all of you. Go read somewhere else. Bring the books back with you to our next class."

He stalked out of the room, leaving us looking at each other in amazement. Was this really one of our teachers? We had to study these three books without instruction for the rest of the week? At least in this, I had the exact same hand dealt to me as everyone else. I could study just as quickly as any of them – although going somewhere else to do it would certainly claw into my time.

I opened the first book, determined to stay and read what I could. Scuffling chairs and feet and chatter were quickly blocked out by the book. I'd started with *Jogler's Kingdoms, Regions and Unknown Lands*. It was the thickest book of the three, but it launched into excitement from the first word:

The tales of the five kingdoms and the lands beyond are not for those faint of heart or dim of wits. Read with caution for wisdom may be found in these accounts and by them, ye may learn not to repeat the mistakes of olde.

I felt the tingle in my bones of a tale to be told. I shivered slightly, curled my feet up under me and read on. Eventually, the room quieted, although I heard the furtive sounds of someone else nearby. After what felt like only minutes, the light grew dim so that the words were hard to make out and I was forced to close my book and look up. I surfaced back to the present time like a diver from the depths and I saw a boy sitting opposite to me holding his books against his chest like they were a newborn lamb or kitten needing the warmth of a body close by.

"You're Amel Leafbrought." He was about my age with curling dark hair and a sad expression around his eyes. In the faint light, it was hard to tell much more about him except that his skin was paler than mine and it glowed in the half-light.

"Did the crutch give it away?" I asked, fishing a leather thong out of my pocket to tie the books together so they could be managed with one hand. I was used to keeping string or leather thongs on my person for this purpose.

He laughed and I smiled with him. Had I found the only other person here with a sense of humor?

"I'm Tamas Dawes."

I smiled shyly but realized he wouldn't be able to see my expression in the fading light. "It's nice to meet you."

"You must be very studious."

"Why is that?"

"You read through dinner and it's almost curfew bell."

Disappointment surged through me. I would have liked more of that amazing food. My belly growled at the thought.

"Maybe I should have said something." He laughed again and I liked his laugh.

"If it's almost curfew bell then I should get moving," I said, settling my crutch and heading out of the classroom. "How does everyone else seem to know the schedule here? No one told me what the bells mean or where I should be for them."

The moon was rising over the delta below and silver edged the landscape and alcoves of Dragon School. Above the cliff-side, tall spires rose like icicles sticking the wrong way up. Towers of the Dragon Riders. Children sketched those in the dirt of our village even though we'd never seen them. We followed the ledge together, towards the ladder.

"It follows the Castelan schedule. If you grew up noble you know it by heart. First bell is waking, second is meditation, third breakfast, fourth is first duty, fifth lunch, sixth is second duty, seventh supper, eighth is third duty, ninth songs, tenth curfew and then the night bells."

"They ring bells at night?"

"For the night watches or the evening meditations and patrols."

"So, everyone else knows what to do because they were raised to this and it's only the details that change?"

We reached the ladder and I slotted my crutch into place on my back. Tamas seemed content to wait for me.

"Exactly. Details are given at meals right now while we're trainees. It changes after First Flight, but things are informal this first week. The Dragon Riders don't like to get too attached."

"You must be noble, then," I said as we scaled the ladder. It seemed even more frightening to climb the cliff side in the dark of night. "Since you know the schedule."

"You'd think so, wouldn't you?"

We arrived at the girls' dorms and he paused for a moment. "It was a pleasure to meet you, Amel Leafbrought. I was hoping to make a friend my first week here."

"Does that mean we're friends?"

"We are if you want to be." Was that a twinkle in his eye or a glint of moonlight?

"I could use a friend." I was too shy to wait for his response. What if he took back his offer? I hurried into the dorm and almost collided with Starie.

"Watch it, peasant. And watch who you're spending your time with. People who start as servants can always go back to that position."

What did she mean by that?

Chapter Eight

THE NEXT MORNING, I used what I learned to get ready and in the right place in time for breakfast. The dining hall was loud with chatter and hot clattering dishes. Steam filled the air as a serving girl pulled the silver lid off a dish of eggs and set them on the long serving table. Metal pitchers of hot teas were quickly refilled as soon as they ran dry by a series of servants arriving with cast-iron kettles. The cold air of the fresh morning fueled my appetite and smelling yeasty goodness in the air as a Dragon Rider nearby broke open a fresh-baked roll made my mouth water.

Even arriving right at the bell, I was only one among many pouring into the great hall. Dragon Riders were outdoors people and they were morning people. More people than in my entire village – than in all the five villages of my home – lived in Dragon School and they all ate together, except the servants, of course.

Off to one side of the hall, I caught a glimpse of the boy I'd met last night, Tamas, talking to a white-clad servant. His arms were crossed like he was upset about something. Should I try to help somehow? His body language suggested that he didn't want to be interrupted.

I hurried to the trainee table, gathering up two of the hot crusty rolls from a basket and piece of fruit. I couldn't afford to linger here if I was going to make it up to Tack and Stables in time for the morning lesson.

"Sit down, you're blocking my view," Starie was her usual pleasant self as she slid onto the bench beside me. Space was limited at the trainee table, or I doubted she would choose to sit near me. Perhaps she wasn't a morning person like the other Dragon Riders.

"Trainees." Grandis Dantriet strode up to our table. "Lesson changes this morning. Due to yesterday's events, Tack and Stables will be abbreviated. Clean your dragon's stable quickly and carefully. You will have only fifteen minutes to finish. After that, you will go topside to watch a display of skill by the Inducted. I shall meet you there."

He strode off, head high and businesslike. For a school, these people certainly didn't seem to enjoy a lot of talking or lecturing. Every single one of them was a person of action – fresh air, exercise, sharp words and good food - that was my impression of Dragon Riders.

I tore a bite out of my chunk of bread and tucked the rest in my pockets, heading for the door. I would have loved to stay and sit for a while. The cheerful bustle of the dining hall brought back memories of home, and the combination of cool morning air and steaming piles of food was hard to resist. It would be fun to sit in a corner, sipping tea and listening to all the conversations, but if I wanted to get my dragon's stable clean in time, I would need to hurry.

I made it up the ladder just as the bell for first duty was sounding. At least I knew what the bells meant now! I'd love to see some of them ringing. There was more than one that rang, but I didn't know where they were. With the echoing of the cliff face, they could be anywhere.

You're back.

I smiled as I heard his voice in my mind. I was getting used to Raolcan. Did he like it here?

I'm a prisoner.

Of course. I should have remembered that.

But no more than you are. You can't ever leave either, can you?

I couldn't, but I was a peasant girl with a bad leg. Raolcan was a massive, powerful dragon.

We have a treaty with the Dominion. It is an old bond. Our part of the treaty is to provide you with dragons to ride.

Are you saying that you volunteered?

Who would choose a life under the rule of another? But someone had to go, and I have no mate, no children. I will not be missed as much as others would.

Do you miss your home?

I miss everything.

I missed my home, too. If he agreed to come, then why did they tie him up? It seemed needlessly cruel. He was no brute beast.

Thank you.

Why did he thank me?

For your trust. You shouldn't trust dragons, though. I will rend and flame as much as any other.

But not me. I knew he wouldn't try to harm me. He'd admitted as much.

We shall see. I am still a dragon.

But he was also my friend. And we were in this together. I thought I could feel him smile as I hobbled along the ledge towards his alcove. I wondered what it would be like to embark on this journey with anyone else but Raolcan. Imagine if I were Dannil whose dragon bit his arm right off? I shuddered, peering into the alcoves as I went.

There was Daedru's golden dragon, its mane shimmering in the dawn light. He yawned, his massive mouth opening so wide that I could step inside and my head would barely brush the roof of his mouth. I shuddered and moved on.

Once I neared the Reds, I saw Savette's Eeamdor, but I didn't near his pen. His sleek red scales shone in the sun like polished glass, but he was gouting flames out the door of his alcove. I timed my passing carefully to avoid them.

When I reached the Green stables, I saw a chalkboard with Tamas' name written on it beside the name 'Ieffban.' So, Tamas was going to be Green if he prevailed. What sort of dragon had he been given? The alcove was dark and the door had thick woolen hangings over it. Perhaps Tamas really was rich of he could afford those. They had no embroidery or fancy dye work like the other curtains. Curious, I pulled back the draping to look inside.

The moment that light filled the alcove I was slammed against the alcove wall. Sulfurous breath filled my lungs and I choked on the fumes. Something hard and sharp scraped across the wall beside my face. I steeled myself and looked. It was a massive claw. The other claw was on the other side of my face, while the webbing spread under my jaw. I was pinned against the wall, at Ieffban's mercy. Should I scream? What would be the point? Death was only moments away. I would not lose my dignity in my last moments.

Halt. Raolcan's voice flooded my mind like a barked order. Halt what? I was pinned here. I could go nowhere. *She is mine.*

The claws didn't move. But the pressure of the webbing eased a little. Should I try to duck under his grip? Even if I could, I wouldn't be able to run fast enough to flee him – not with my leg. I drew in a wavering breath.

Touch her and I will shred you to scraps and then burn what remains of you until the fat bubbles out.

Well, that really painted a picture. Delightful, Raolcan. You should be a poet in your spare time.

I clenched my jaw in pain as the sound of fingernails on a slate – only magnified times fifty – filled my ears. The claws scraped at the wall and then I was released as quickly as I'd been caught. I fell to the floor, scrambling on hands and knee for my crutch. I found it, wobbled to my feet, and dashed out the door as quickly as a leg and crutch could carry me. I didn't stop to look back. Who cared why the alcove was different or what Ieffban looked like?

He's not nearly as good looking as I am.

Thank you for saving me, Raolcan. Really, what would I do without you?

Die. But let's not dwell on that.

As I rushed from the cage I smacked straight into a Dragon Rider. I stumbled, but he caught my elbows as my crutch clattered again to the floor. Light gleamed off a shaven head and dark eyes assessed me.

"Well, you're certainly curious enough to be Purple, that's for sure. Would you like to explain why you were in another trainee's alcove?" The look in Leng's eye was danger and curiosity rolled up over each other.

"I wanted to know why the curtains were so thick over his alcove."

Leng barked a laugh. "It's a gift from his family. Servants of Dragon School can choose at age sixteen whether to join the servant ranks or try to be a Dragon Rider themselves. Tamas chose to try the harder path. His family doesn't have much to help him except for this – dark curtains are said to keep the dragon docile and manageable. They are trying to keep him alive."

"Docile? I don't think it's working." Still, it was incredibly sweet of them. I thought back to the servant talking so intensely with him in the dining hall. A relative, perhaps? His mother or aunt? And he knew what the bells meant, not because he was a Castelan, but because he grew up here.

Leng laughed again. Either he found everything humorous, or just everything about me.

"Don't laugh. He nearly bit my face off. And why are all the dragons male? Where are the girl dragons?"

This time his laugh came out a snort before he calmed down enough to answer. "Female dragons are larger and extremely elusive. Our arrangement with the Ha'drazen – the Dragon Queen – is for males only. They choose which ones and send them to a specific location where we round them up and bring them here. They are all young and most of them are completely wild until we gentle them."

"It seems like a strange thing to do to a creature that can think as clearly as we can. Shouldn't they be free to live life as they see fit?"

His gaze wandered off into the distance and his expression grew sad. "Are you free? Am I?"

"You looked like the freest man in the world yesterday. I saw you fly high in the sky and then leap off your dragon like thistledown flying in the breeze."

His smile had returned. "Give it a week and you'll do the same."

I felt a pang in my chest. I'd never leap like that, no matter how much I succeeded here.

"I'm glad that you'll be Purple, little sister," he said with a smile. "Your curiosity marks you as a good choice for our Color. Follow that up with some wisdom and you might go far."

He strode off so abruptly that I had to take a moment to catch my breath. Dragon Riders sure were strange people. They were as wild and predatory as the creatures they rode. Although I was beginning to have doubts about whether we should be riding dragons at all.

At least, if I must be owned, I am owned by someone who understands she has no right to my service.

I felt a chill in my spine at Raolcan's thoughts. They were jagged and filled with emotion. Thank you for saving me, Raolcan. I owe you a debt.

I will consider it paid if you always remember that we are equals. You do not command this dragon. We are partners together.

Chapter Nine

WHEN RAOLCAN'S ALCOVE was clean to his specifications, I joined the line of trainees headed up the ladder to the top of the butte. They were in good spirits despite the events of yesterday and jests rang out from those waiting for a turn on the ladder. Savette arrived, breathless, behind me.

"Are you okay?" I asked her.

"Of course, I am." She looked irritated, so I left her alone. She was a puzzle: kind one minute, distant the next. It was like she was working from a code that was entirely different from my own and completely opaque. I left her alone. Maybe I'd figure her out eventually.

The line moved forward and I studied the pulley on the wall. This one was rigged with a long board and a couple of block pulleys for belaying heavy loads up the cliff. I squinted at it, trying to work out how they operated the system. If they could belay heavy loads up, then I could go up and down that way, although the thought still left butterflies in my belly. If I was honest, though, I knew that I'd never sit down for a meal again if I didn't figure out a quicker way to go up and down between levels.

By the time I reached the top of the ladder I was breathless and Savette – the only person behind me – had taken on an air of extreme patience. I didn't know what made me feel worse; the insults of others or her longsuffering attitude. I thought it might be her. After all, it was easy to retaliate against insults, harder to ask someone to stop waiting so aggressively.

I gasped at my first look at 'topside.' I'd expected scraggly vegetation and ragged rocks. I should have used my imagination more. A crystal-clear lake spread across the top of the mountain – the source, no doubt, of the water that flowed into Dragon School. Tall spires of various heights and designs encrusted the edge of the bluffs. They bore one thing in common – long branches spread from each one to provide a perch for dragons and silken banners flapped in the wind.

Between two spires, a wide semi-circle of rock was hewed into steps – or seating, I realized after a moment. There was room on it for hundreds and our tiny wave of trainees were huddled together on the lower few steps. At each end of the semi-circle, a dragon was carved, posed in an aggressive posture as if ready to attack whatever came near. It was an imposing sight. I would have been nervous to address so large a crowd at the best of times, but when you added carved dragons and a cliff at your back, you'd need nerves of steel to speak to the people here.

"Take your seats." Grandis Leman stood a little to one side, looking much happier here in the open air, but his dark expression was still black as night. What made him so moody? Beside him was Grandis Dantriet, looking off into the horizon.

"We are just about ready," Grandis Dantriet announced as Savette and I hurried to take our seats. "Call the Inducted, Grandis Leman."

Leman pulled a silver whistle the length of his hand out of a pocket and carefully piped a three-note call. From behind one of the carved dragons, the Inducted ran out. Their close-fitting gray leather outfits made them look more like a team than our ragged band of trainees and they ran in a perfect line. They must train together physically as well as over books. I felt a pang as I realized that there would never be a time that I could run in a line like that. I couldn't even avoid holding Savette back on the way up the ladder.

They lined up along the cliff edge and Grandis Leman stepped out in front of them.

"Are you ready to be tested on maneuvers, Inducted?" he asked.

"Yes, Dragon Rider!" they chorused together. Strange, they didn't call him Grandis.

"Prepare to mount your dragons!"

I looked around with confusion and noted that the rest of my wave were just as confused until I finally followed Grandis Dantriet's gaze. He watched the horizon, and then a moment later a chain of multicolored dragons were visible. Led by a Dragon Rider in black leathers and a Green dragon, and tailed by a second Green, the chain of dragons flew towards us with the speed of a strong west wind.

Along the cliff's edge, the Inducted stood so close to the drop that I feared they would fall over the edge. If they stood so close, where would the dragons land? I stood, without thinking, my heart in my throat. What were they thinking? This was far too dangerous! The dragons were so close now that I thought they were diving straight for the semi-circle, until they wheeled at the last second, curving to swoop parallel to the cliff face.

The lead dragon dove beneath the edge of the cliff, disappearing from view, his green silken scarves fluttering in the wind. Directly behind him was a saddled white dragon with no rider. That dragon dipped below the cliff edge and then – lightning fast- one of the Inducted leapt from the cliff.

"No!" I gasped. I'd just witnessed a suicide. Horror gripped my chest, dark and thick. He would be falling through the air, falling to his death. Someone needed to dive one of those dragons down and save him. Why was no one screaming? Why weren't they moving? They had to hurry!

And then another Inducted leapt, and another, all down the line of Inducted. My mouth went dry and my heart raced a thousand miles a second. I didn't mean to clap a hand over my mouth but it went up on its own, clamping my scream inside. What madness was this?

"And that," Grandis Dantriet said proudly, "is how you mount a dragon. Who wants to be first?"

Chapter Ten

THE INDUCTED WHEELED their dragons around and up, climbing so we could see them stretched out in a ragged line. They struggled to fly in sync with one another, instead turning reluctant dragons more slowly and aggressive ones far too quickly. I couldn't make out particulars from so far away, but I got the sense that they were still nervous and it made them more clumsy.

Even with that in mind, they were spectacular. They flew low over our seats, so we could see every scale on the bellies of the dragons. Spectacular was too weak a word to describe the dragons' movements. They'd start bunched up, filled with energy longing to be released, and then they'd explode forward, their wings shuddering as they flapped them down, muscles flexing and skin stretching out along the wings. Glittering eyes and shining scales glinted in the sunlight and thick leather straps ringed the dragons' bellies and shoulders, holding Inducted tightly into their saddles. How in the world did they keep from getting motion sick? I was guessing that as many people lost those grand breakfasts we ate as not during the training process.

The dragons turned a corner, fringed wings and scintillating tails displaying in every color and variation from ombre golds to albino whites. I gasped in pleasure, still standing as I had been in my shock. It felt wrong to sit for such a grand display. To fly like that – what a dream come true! Even if it meant leaping over the side of a cliff? I wasn't sure about that. I got sick bubbles in my belly and hot fear sliced through the backs of my thighs when I thought about leaping over the side of the cliff. What if Raolcan didn't catch me? What if I slipped off the saddle? What if I couldn't leap correctly because of my leg and I fell too close to the side and smacked the cliff?

"The art of gentling a dragon goes back eight generations in our land." Grandis Dantriet's voice cut through the ambient noise with power. "Our ancestors have taught us the fine skill of bonding with a dragon and then riding him. It is only after your First Flight that you will be eligible for induction into our ranks. As you can see, it's more challenging than you may have guessed." Grandis Dantriet grinned, the lines in his weathered face deepening into the passion of someone doing what they loved best in the world. "Every wave of Dragon Rider trainees goes through Induction in the same way that you will. First, you choose a dragon and with that, a potential Color. Next, you watch the students in the wave before yours ride their dragons. If what you have seen is too much for you, there is always room in the servant ranks. There is no shame in serving others. It's a good life of hard work and purposeful duty. You may choose it at any time in this process. We want none in our ranks who do not truly wish to be here. So, choose wisely. Choose the path you wish to take. Tonight, the bonding commences. Once you have bonded with your dragon you will be forced to continue on your path much more forcefully. We will not have dragons wasted and a dragon will only bond to one person. This is your last chance to easily choose a different path. You have until sunset to make your choice."

Should I feel grateful to have a choice? Somehow, it made things harder. I'd come here so that I wouldn't be a burden on my family. I hadn't realized servanthood would be an option. A life as a servant here with plentiful food, a warm bed, and useful chores was everything I could have hoped for - before. Now, after meeting Raolcan - after watching that glorious display – I wasn't sure that I could walk away from it. Could I just settle for something less? Quit without trying? It felt like quitting even if it was safer and made more sense. Imagine if I succeeded? Who needed to walk or run quickly when they could fly?

"We all know what you should choose, peasant girl." I heard the whisper, but I didn't turn around. "And I think you do, too. All you do is hold up the line."

I colored in shame. It wouldn't hurt so much if it wasn't true. I didn't turn around because I didn't want to confirm my suspicions. Only Savette had been held up on the ladder, and I was starting to think that we were friends. I couldn't bear to look back and see her lovely face mocking me.

"Two things happen tonight. First, you will go through the bonding ritual." Grandis Dantriet was addressing us again. Beside him, Grandis Leman looked bored, his eyes occasionally trailing the dragons still looping around us in a ragged ring. "And secondly, you will place a secret vote in this jar." He held up a clay jar with a lid. "The first person of every wave to mount their dragon suffers a significant disadvantage. We have lost over half of those who have tried first. It is, however, a great honor to succeed. First Rider is a title we respect. Choose the First Rider of your wave carefully."

It took a moment for his words to sink in. Lost? Did he mean... dead? By the looks on the faces around me, he did.

"In the past, we have drawn names randomly for the dangerous task of First Rider. But, this time we have decided to let you vote. We start a new tradition with you."

The dragons finished their circle and dove over our seats again, this time spinning so that their riders were upside down and then right side up again. I gasped at the thought of doing that myself. It made my head spin just thinking about it.

"You have until tonight to make both your decisions. I suggest you take that time to meditate, rest and eat well. You will need all your energy and mental acuity. Bonding will take a lot out of you and the choice you make will determine your future. May the sun shine on you. We will convene at the stables at eighth bell. If you are late, or do not arrive, then your decision has been made. You will continue on as a servant of Dragon School. Whatever your choice, we embrace your service."

The two Grandis turned and left, leaving us silent in the stands.

After a moment, we looked at one another and Starie stood, bumping me with her shoulder as she walked by and stating loudly, "I'll be voting for you, cripple. Unless you choose the right thing tonight."

Jael followed her, shrugging at me as he passed.

I bit back a retort. If I wanted to prove her wrong I'd have all the chance I needed soon enough. What hurt worse than Starie's words were the other trainees. None of them would look at me as they walked by. Not even Savette or Tamas. If I chose to bond with Raolcan tonight, it was clear whose name they were going to write down on their papers. A choice to try to be a Dragon Rider would mean the task of First Rider, too, and with it a fifty percent chance of death. How badly did I really want to ride a dragon?

Chapter Eleven

BY THE TIME I'D DESCENDED the ladder to the stable levels there was no sign of anyone else. Likely, they were doing as they were told and resting, meditating and eating. The thought of going to those huge dorms with every eye on me made my stomach lurch. I didn't need more people who doubted me to fill me with self-doubt. I made my way along the ledge – although not too close to the alcoves. I didn't need a repeat of this morning. I still felt a bit shaky when I thought of that Green dragon. Imagine leaping onto the back of a creature like that! Would it shake you off? Would it try to? How quickly could you strap yourself into the saddle?

I stopped beside one alcove where a saddle was hanging on a peg. The complicated straps culminated in a wide harness for the rider, including a waist strap and shoulder and thigh loops. It looked like it would take a long time to strap on, and when Leng had leapt off his dragon onto the ledge, he hadn't been wearing it. Did most Dragon Riders wear them, or only trainees?

I walked away, letting my mind wander over the idea of leaping – on in my case more like dropping – over the edge of a cliff and onto a dragon. I could envision what it would take to decide to do it. I could envision landing hard on the scaly, slippery saddle. What then? Would I strap in? Would Raolcan try to buck me off?

Try? If I wanted you off you'd be off in a heartbeat.

I was at his alcove without realizing it and as I pulled back the curtain I saw that he wasn't penned in on the side of the alcove like he was when we came to clean the stalls.

I'm as free as they let me be between those cleanings. Free to sit here and be miserable and bored. Why have you come?

"I have until tonight to decide if I will be a Dragon Rider or a servant." Speaking out loud seemed more respectful than in my head when we were side by side.

And is there any question in your mind?

"The others think I will die dropping over the side of the cliff to mount you."

Always a possibility.

I swallowed down a surge of fear. Thinking it was one thing. Saying it out loud and having someone agree was something else entirely. I blinked back hot tears forming in my eyes.

"They also think you'll just buck me right off."

Dragons are not kind. Especially those facing a lifetime of slavery.

So, I wasn't wrong to envision that. "What worries me most is that slavery thing. If I agree to be your rider, won't I be adding to your slavery?"

If it isn't you, then it will be someone else.

"What if it is me and then I die? What happens to you then?"

He didn't answer for a long time, so I sat down beside him and put a hand on his smooth cheek. His scales were hot, but not burning. Apparently magic kept him penned here, though there was no visible sign of it.

I can see the magical bonds. If you are bound to me, you will see them, too. You'll see a lot of new things that you can't see now.

"Why?"

Because the bond will tap you into my magic and with that, give you eyes to see the magic all around you.

That sounded exciting. I hated the thought that there were things to see that I was blind to.

You are blind to many things.

"What will it mean for you to be bound to me?" He still didn't answer, so I tried a different question. "What do you want."

I want to be free. The answer was lightning-fast.

"What can I do to give you that?" I couldn't even see his magical bonds. I certainly couldn't loosen them for him.

Nothing. I am a slave now, forever. Choose to bond with me and I will be your slave.

That sounded horrible. I'd never wanted anyone or anything to be enslaved to me. Perhaps, I should say no. Perhaps, it was better to work in the kitchens here than to force this magnificent creature to serve me.

You should choose to bond with me.

I was more confused than ever. He wanted me to choose him and yet that would mean slavery for him? That made no sense. I was more confused than ever.

Raolcan closed his eyes and set his head down on the ground. Was he asleep? I sat for a long time in silence, weighing my options. I really didn't want to be a servant. I really did want to be a Dragon Rider. The more I thought about it, the more

I was willing to try that terrifying First Flight – or at least, I thought I was – but what about Raolcan? What about his freedom? It wasn't right for him to be a slave and if I chose to ride him that's what he would be. He was being very closemouthed about the whole thing. Did he know something that I didn't know? Was he keeping it from me? It seemed this decision was mine alone to make and he would not be helping me.

Whatever I chose, his life would change. It felt like too much responsibility for one crippled peasant girl. I'd have to be very wise in my choice. My heart squeezed in my chest at the look of his sleeping form. If only I knew for sure what was best for him. The responsibility made me feel sleepy. I leaned against Raolcan, closing my eyes. I'd just rest here for a moment. Only for a moment...

Chapter Twelve

I AWOKE TO A ROUGH hand on my shoulder and looked up into a shocked expression. Leng Shardson's unshaven face was pale in the afternoon sun. His gaze flicked back and forth between Raolcan and I. Had I noticed before that he was an attractive man? His narrow lips were parted and his sharp, bird-of-prey gaze was a lot like Raolcan's. Maybe proximity to dragons made you become more like them.

"What are you doing?" His words were breathless, his eyes full of awe.

I rubbed my eyes. "I think I fell asleep."

"Against an ungentled dragon?" There was a burr in his voice. Was he worried for me? He needed to trust Raolcan like I did. It wasn't fair that everyone mistrusted him just because of who he was. I understood what it was like to have everyone misjudge you.

"He's not going to hurt me."

Raolcan's sides swelled as he drew in a breath. The same breath snorted out with a slight sulfur smell as he slept.

"I heard they were bonding your wave tonight," he said.

"Where do you go on your dragon every day?" Maybe if I changed the subject I wouldn't have to talk about my impending choice.

He smiled slightly. "Purples are messengers. We fly from one place to another bearing messages. I've been stationed with Dragon School for now, and that means daily missives to the twelve towers. It's boring work, but someone has to do it."

"You don't like delivering messages?"

"I love my Color and I'm dedicated to our work but this is a tame posting. I'd rather be almost anywhere else – or at least that's how I felt before."

Before what? Had he met someone? A lover, a friend, a wife? That would change a person's mind. Or maybe he'd been promoted. Perhaps someday, if I succeeded, I'd be complaining about the boredom of my post. It seemed almost too good to be true – as far away as a distant land or a desperate hope.

"You should eat. Bonding will take a lot out of you." He'd been crouching beside me but now he stood, offering me a hand.

I took his hand and let him help me up, but there was no way I was going to the dining hall. "I don't want to eat with everyone right now. I'm happier here."

"You're happier in the stables?" He seemed pleased by that. "There's food in Alhskibi's alcove. Come on."

I followed his lead, but he walked companionably beside me until we got to the Purple alcoves. The carving around the doors was in whorls and swooping designs, like wind. I ran my fingers over the swirls closest to me. They were gorgeous.

"The marks of the Purple," Leng said with a smile. "We are the swiftest of all the riders, so our symbol is the wind. Swift, lean and truthful. Our Color hosts races often. Let's hope you can ride fast."

I hoped I could ride at all. It was marvelous to think of being part of a Color – of having others like me in a common goal – but it wasn't making my decision any easier. It would probably be kinder to Raolcan if I didn't bond with him – if I let him be free. He claimed that he would never be free, that they'd just give him to someone else. So perhaps he would only be free if I was bonded to him and then walked away."

"What happens to a bonded dragon if his rider leaves?" I asked, as Leng stopped in front of a silk-curtained alcove.

"Dies, you mean? The dragon will die, too. Your lives are intertwined after the bonding."

My eyes widened and my throat felt tight. If I died on that first flight, Raolcan would die, too? "What if the rider simply walked away."

Leng's eyes narrowed and his hand hovered over the name chalked beside the alcove – *Ahlskibi*.

"I hope you aren't thinking of doing that."

Was I? "I'm only curious."

"It's not so simple. People don't walk away. If you tried, your dragon would die from that, too."

"So, once they arrive here they're slaves forever?" I sighed.

He frowned and took my hand. "There's something different about you and Raolcan. I can see that already. Believe me when I tell you, the best thing for him is you. You can't free him by walking away. Do you understand?"

I nodded, but I didn't understand. Wouldn't it be better for him if there was no me? An able-bodied rider could offer him so much more.

"Let me tell you a secret." He leaned in so close that I could feel his breath on my neck as he whispered to me. It gave me little chills and made it hard to concentrate. "Riding dragons might be physical work but a big spirit matters more than what you can do with your body."

He drew back, and then gracefully opened the curtain to the alcove. Behind it, a magnificent purple dragon with a frill around its head stood, rearing back slightly at our presence. Leng smiled and something wordless passed between them. Could they speak to one another as Raolcan and I could?

Of course.

I gasped and stepped back. That was Ahlskibi in my head! He spoke to me! And now he seemed to be laughing at me.

"Let me introduce you to Ahlskibi – my dragon partner," Leng said, crossing to a leather bag and pulling out flatbread and dried meat. "Let's eat. You must be hungry."

We took a seat on the edge of the ledge so that our feet dangled over the side of the cliff and he broke off bread and meat and handed them to me. I was hungrier than I'd realized and a little giddy from the heights, the possibilities and eating lunch with a Real Dragon Rider. Too shy to speak, I concentrated on the food. All the Purple dragons spoke into their rider's minds! That was amazing. Eventually, I took the last bite and found Leng's warm gaze hovering on me.

"Good luck tonight and tomorrow, Amel Leafbrought. Some of us were born to this life and I think you are one of us."

Me? Born to this? The peasant girl with the useless leg? I bit my tongue in surprise and tasted blood. He couldn't be serious.

"I have more messages to deliver. I hope that when I return I find you wearing gray." He stood and offered me a hand again and I accepted. "If you stand by the chalkboard you can watch. Maybe you'll pick up a tip or two."

I hobbled over to the sign, eyes wide as he deftly pulled a saddle from the wall, cocked his head at Ahlskibi and then threw the saddle over his back. Ahlskibi stood, and Leng darted under him, cinching girth bands and closing buckles with practiced hands. It was less than a minute before he retreated out from under him. I moved to look closer, but Ahlskibi's head darted out, teeth bared at me. I stepped back quickly. Apparently, even being on speaking terms wasn't enough to mean you could go near a dragon.

"Stay well back," Leng warned, his expression hard. I took another step back and then something I couldn't discern changed and Ahlskibi leapt forward, launching himself off the cliffs and out towards the horizon. He wheeled in a slow arc.

"Once they're gentled you can jump on after you put the saddle on, but I thought you should watch me mount the way you'll have to," Leng said. His expression was serious, but there was a look of hope – or something similar – in his eyes. "Watch closely. I'll work slowly for you."

Ahlskibi circled back towards us and Leng shot me a final grin before running towards the cliff and leaping off. I scrambled to the edge and watched him fly through the air, his limbs splayed in an exaggerated manner. He was going to miss Ahlskibi! And then the dragon was suddenly under him, dipping as Leng's weight dropped on him.

Leng pulled the belt from where it was tucked behind the saddle up to his waist and fastened it with two quick motions.

He slid his arms in the harness and clipped the buckle over his chest in a single graceful motion. Ahlskibi's wings rose, caught the wind and then with a powerful motion he launched forward, gripping the air and propelling up into the sky. I gasped at the glorious power of his movements. It was hard not to long to be a part of that beauty.

When they were nothing but a dot on the horizon I finally turned away. I hoped Leng was right and that I'd see them again. There was something special about those two. They were kind to someone like me that everyone else only tolerated – or worse, despised. I wanted to eat dried meat and flatbread with Leng every day and talk about dragons. Maybe that was what being Inducted was like. Maybe that wasn't as far off as I feared.

Chapter Thirteen

I WENT BACK TO THE dorms, grateful to find most of the other female trainees resting or meditating. It only took a moment to slip a fresh set of clothes out of my bag and slip into the back. Come what may, I planned to be clean and in fresh clothes. The shower was heavenly, and I felt so fresh and new that I braved the dining hall next. A wave of nerves passed over me as I sat and I barely managed to swallow down two bites of roast chicken and some water. At least the rest of my wave was just as consumed with what came next. They barely noticed that I was there at all.

Around us, Dragon School carried on. Chuckles and smiles from the other tables and loud conversation, occasionally broken up by the sober expression of one of the Grandis made everyone else seem indifferent to our plight. But no wonder. Hadn't they all done the very same thing we were about to do and lived to tell about it?

I slipped out of the dining hall early, grateful for the cool breeze against my sweaty brow. I hadn't expected to be so nervous, but it was eating at me. The bell rang and a new kind of fear stabbed through me. I needed to be up top as quickly as the others but I didn't have the time to get there and now the bell was ringing!

I sped towards the stairs, painfully aware that trainees beside me were easily passing me at only an average walking speed. I bit my lip. If I was late, all was lost – for Raolcan and me, at least.

What was that down the path? Was that what I thought it was? A lift on cables and pulleys sat beside the kitchen, loaded with a pair of crates still to be unloaded. Over the edge of the crate, I saw eggs packed in straw. It would be a simple enough thing to move the light crates off and stand on the lift myself, but to sway on an unstable lift hundreds of yards above the ground and with no way to get down if things went wrong – could I even do it?

There was no time to lose. I hurried over, dragged the crates off, thankful that they were light enough for me to move and then crawled onto the wooden bench suspended between two cables. My stomach fluttered as the plank swayed under my weight, but I gripped the cable attached to the pulley, jammed my crutch between my good thigh and the bench and wrapped that leg tightly around the board while the other hung dead on the other side. It was now or never. I hauled hard on the cable, my shoulders screaming with the effort, but the board shot upwards, the pulleys easily magnifying my efforts. It was easy to draw the rope through so I was able to pull hand over hand all the way up from the dining hall level to topside.

A silver whistle greeted me as, huffing and exhausted, I pulled myself off the swaying board and onto the firm rock. It felt good to grip the rock and know it was firm under my hands and knees. I needed a cold drink of water and a chance to lie down, but then I would miss my opportunity. Gritting my teeth against nausea and nerves, I hauled up on my crutch and fell in behind Tamas who was last in line.

"Best wishes on your bonding," I said to him. There was no need to hold a grudge for his distant behavior. We could still be friends. He didn't reply, but maybe it was just nerves. We were all nervous, weren't we?

"Welcome," Grandis Dantriet's words rang out over the cliffside. The sun hung low in the sky, painting his white braids and loose hair an orangey hue that suited him. "We gather for bonding between dragon and rider trainee. This is your last chance to bow out of your commitment to the dragon you chose. Do any of you chose to take that option now?"

My hands shook as everyone looked back at me. They just assumed that I would crack now that the pressure was on. Why did they think that I wasn't up to the task? Was a ruined leg really enough to destroy your entire future? I didn't think it should be. I stiffened my shoulders and held my head high. No flinching from Amel Leafbrought. If they thought I wasn't worthy then I would just have to show them all that they were wrong about me.

Like a bag of grain falling open and spilling on the ground, Tamas fell to his knees in front of me, head in his hands.

"I can't do it. I thought I could but I can't." His tone sounded strange – like it didn't even belong to him.

"Don't give up now," I whispered. If he could just make it through these two tests he'd have gotten past the hardest part. He just needed a bit more encouragement.

He craned his head back to glare at me, his fingers gripping into the dust on the ground like claws. I gasped at his dark expression. "Shut up, cripple. We all know you aren't going to make it out of this alive. Stop fooling yourself. I won't be an idiot like you." He turned his gaze back to the rest of them. "I know my place. I should never have tried to rise above it."

Grandis Dantriet raised a hand, cutting off comments muttered throughout the group. "The purpose of this ritual warning is for those like Tamas who learn this is not the life for them. Go with our blessing, Tamas. Return to the servants' quarters. Are there any others?"

All eyes were fixed on me as Tamas strode away to the ladders. I felt my face grow hot but as the seconds stretched to minutes, I refused to crumble under their gazes. I wasn't going to give in. They'd all have to watch me fail or succeed on my own effort. I bit my lip and willed myself to be steadfast.

"Very well." Grandis Dantriet scanned our ranks, as if counting us and then gestured to the stands behind him. "Behind these stands, your dragons are arrayed. Our Binder, Grandis Echomeyer, is with them. You will each be bound by magic to your dragon. This gentles them to your touch. They may not listen to your commands, but your own dragon can no longer maim or kill you. Be careful of all other dragons in these stables. Only your bonded dragon is bound to keep from harming you. You will also be bound against harming him. It is the way of the Dragon Riders. Our bonds are sacred and revered. So let it be for the ages."

"So let it be for the ages," the trainees around me replied. Another thing borrowed from the nobles that I knew nothing about, I supposed.

We followed him around the seating area in the ragged line we were in. With every step, my heart hammered louder. Was I making the right choice? I desperately wanted to be a Dragon Rider – it was all I could do to keep images of delivering messages on the back of a grand purple dragon from flooding my mind – but what if it was bad for Raolcan? It was bad enough that he was a slave here. Was I making things worse by choosing him? He'd been cagey when I asked him, unwilling to say one way or the other. Should I have pushed him harder, or was it best simply to take him at his word that this bond was best for him?

As we followed the line of dragons, the trainees peeled off to where their dragon stood. Savette seemed almost to skip towards her red dragon and off toward the end I saw someone leading a green dragon away – Tamas' dragon. I felt a pang at the thought of him kneeling in the dust, giving up his whole future. He didn't need to do that. He shouldn't have done it just because the other students doubted us. I wished I had the chance to tell him that. Maybe I should have been out there helping people be brave this afternoon instead of sleeping in Raolcan's stable and then watching Leng ride off to the horizon. I swallowed back worry and tried to focus on what was ahead. Raolcan? Where are you?

Wait, was that him? Why was he so silent? I didn't hear him in my mind at all. Something wasn't right. It made me feel strange and lonely – like a butterfly on a snowy field. Was he angry? Was he silent in his anger? His golden gaze fixed on mine as if he was trying to communicate silently, but that was just silly. After all, if he wanted to speak to me mind to mind he easily could. I cleared my throat, suddenly uncertain.

I waited as Grandis Echomeyer and Grandis Dantriet worked their way slowly back down the line in the gathering dark. We were stretched too far apart to see what they were doing with each trainee before us. I was almost startled when they finally found me in the dark. Two servants held torches beside the Grandis, outlining everything in dancing orange hues.

"Amel Leafbrought?" Grandis Dantriet said as if he didn't already know it was me.

"Yes." My voice shook a little.

"This is the dragon you chose, Raolcan the Purple?"

"Yes." My voice was clearer now.

"Do you choose to bind with this dragon and be his rider?" Grandis Echomeyer asked. He was slender like all Dragon Riders but stooped with age and his skin was yellowed and sagging.

"Yes."

"Hold out your hand." His eyes went still, like he'd retreated to another world and then heat flared in my wrist.

I yelped and drew it back at the same moment that Raolcan snorted, flames gouting out of his nostrils. He missed us, but his continued silence cut deep. Was he angry at me? Was I making the right choice?

A bright white stylized feather appeared on my wrist, and I saw the same feather burning brightly in the twilight against Raolcan's wing. We were marked with an identical sign. I stared at mine in wonder as it faded into a dull glow.

"Different every time." Grandis Echomeyer seemed to beam with pride.

"We're the only ones with this sign?" I liked that, though I still feared Raolcan's silence.

"Yes. Each pair has its own. The magic determines it. You're bound now, and he's gentled to you. Treat him well."

It seemed so informal – so basic – for such an important moment. My eyes went wide with surprise and I would have remained stunned if Grandis Dantriet's voice hadn't broken into my wonder.

"You may write your vote for First Rider now and place it in the jar."

"I don't choose to vote." I was proud of how clear my voice was.

His eyebrows rose. "You realize that it could be you."

I barked a laugh so suddenly that I surprised myself. "Of course, it will be me. That's who everyone else is voting for. I've decided not to make anyone else feel the way I do, with my name on the paper."

"The duty of First Rider is a great honor." His expression was unreadable. "So let it be."

I wasn't surprised when all the rituals were complete and Grandis announced firmly that the vote was unanimous - I would be First Rider the next day. I wasn't surprised when they all trooped away, leaving me to hobble back in their wake. What surprised me – worried me – was the silence from Raolcan. It was like a wind had been blowing for days and was still now. I felt completely abandoned, alone and bereft at his missing voice, and worst of all I feared what it meant for that first flight.

Chapter Fourteen

I WOKE TO THE SOUND of thunder. Rain beat down on the ledge outside the wide window filling the room with the sound. I sat up in the soft bed, trying to shake off sleep. The darkness around me was cloying, trying to pull me back into sweet unconsciousness but the wind thrashed against our dorm and in a flash of lightning I saw a half-dozen girls silhouetted against the light, trying to force the shutters closed.

A bobbing lantern came through the door with a whoosh of wind behind it just as they were finished. Soaked to the skin and irritated looking, Grandis Elfar lit our dorm chandelier with her lantern. Moans and complaints filled the room but she hushed them curtly.

"Enough complaining. Most of you will get to return to your warm beds in a minute, so hush." She waited for quiet before she continued, peering into every cranny of the room to stare down whisperers. "I know that was you, Arielle. Watch it or it's double stable cleaning tomorrow for you. You know that's no idle threat. Now, I'm here for the newest wave of trainees. Front and center."

I climbed awkwardly from my bunk and joined the handful of recruits from my wave. Grandis Elfar grimaced at me, or maybe it was at all of us.

"We've received an urgent message from the Dominion Capitol. The part pertaining to you reads as follows." She pulled out a thick sheaf of paper and began to read. "To that end, all training shall now be expedited. Upon the receiving of this message any trainees who have not completed First Flight by morning shall be removed from Dragon School. Inducted and above shall be trained at the most demanding pace possible for the fulfillment of obligations..."

We gasped.

"Does that mean we're being reduced to servants without even a chance?" Starie protested. "I'm a High Castelan. You can't do this to me!"

"Hush, child," Grandis Elfar looked tired and frustrated rolled into one. "No one is against you in this. It is our hope that we can fulfill the Dominar's decree while retaining all of you, but time is urgent." She ran a hand over her face, as if wiping away the exhaustion. "Usually you have a solid week to prepare for your First Flight. We act as though your First Flight will come before you are ready but honestly, we make sure each of you has what they need to make success probable if you set your mind to the work and really want to do it."

"You do?" Savette gasped.

One of the Initiates behind her snickered, but Grandis Elfar waved a hand in irritation. "Of course, we do. This is a school, not an abattoir. Do you really think we take the maiming and death of students lightly? Of course not. But we must test, test, test or you will never be ready to be real Dragon Riders. Only those of tough spirit and iron spine are ready for the rigors of this life. It is our job to ready you and that can't be achieved gently. But tonight, we must force your First Flight before you are ready, and if all of you make an attempt, we will lose some." Her jaw line stood out as she clenched her teeth, her mouth drawing a grim line before she spoke again. "We do not wish to throw you all in the servant ranks. Many of you are of noble blood. You have the potential to be more than dishwashers and launderers. Make no mistake, we do not push you into this trial. Better to be a boot polisher than a smear on the rocks below." She moved her penetrating gaze from one person to the next, as if to impress on us the image of spattered rocks. "But the choice is yours. The First Flight must be completed before dawn or none of you will be allowed to stay on as recruits. You will all pack your things and move five levels below to the servants' halls. Those who complete First Flight will be initiates. Just like that. No other tests."

"It's storming out there," one of the girls from our wave said in a small voice. I couldn't help but agree, fear welling up in my own heart at the thought of slippery saddles and driving rains to contend with on top of everything else.

Grandios Elfar sighed. "And it's dark. Tonight is a grim night but it is your only chance. If you wish to take that chance, dress. We leave together in five minutes. If you choose to stay as servants, begin packing. Dame Adelle will arrive in ten minutes to shepherd you to the servants' quarters."

I swallowed hard. I could just go now and sleep with the servants, awaking to a good life of being warm and fed and safe here. And if I did that I'd never see Raolcan again. Or Leng. I'd never deliver messages on the back of a Purple dragon. Was this message delivered by a Purple? Only a fool would take their First Flight – as First Rider no less – in the dark, during a storm with death waiting for them.

I turned to my bunk and started to pull my clothing on. I was a fool. I couldn't just walk away. My belly swam with nerves, a sour taste flooding my mouth and my head feeling hot and light. I was going to hurl. I fought down the impulse. I should just pack my things. It would be so easy. I saw one girl already beginning that. She was cautious and wise. She'd probably live to old age with a parcel of grandchildren and worn happy hands. I would probably be a broken hulk on the rocks below by morning. Did birds fly down and tear the flesh from those who fell, or did they let the dragons swoop down and burn them up?

I clenched my jaw hard and fell in line.

"Amel Leafbrought?" Grandis Elfar said.

"Yes?" My hands were shaking so hard that I hid one in the folds of my clothing.

"You understand that time is precious tonight."

I nodded.

"In light of that, you may try a First Flight but we can't wait for you to ascend the ladder. The honor of First Flight will go to another. You will fly your dragon when you arrive topside. Catch up when you can. If you do not ride by dawn your chance is gone."

Honor? I thought it was a punishment. After all, everyone voted for me because they didn't want to be the one to go first. It was horribly humiliating to be singled out a second time over my slow ascent. As if I was somehow a drain on the energy of those around me. Bitterness intermingled with my fear.

"How long until dawn?" I asked.

"Next bell," she said and turned to face the doorway, lantern held high. "Follow me, trainees. Don't fall out of line. If you lose this chance, it's gone forever."

I was already three steps behind when the trainee in front of me was through the door.

Chapter Fifteen

IT WAS SLICK OUTSIDE and my crutch lost purchase and slipped along the rock more times than I could count as I hobbled to the first set of ladders. The bench and pulleys from earlier were gone, not that I thought swaying up on a bench in the middle of a storm was a good idea. Ladders were slippery enough. I gripped the ladder as hard as I could in cold, shaking hands. I was wet to the bone already and starting to feel chilled. Water poured over my face, blurring my vision and the endless drumming of rain against the cliff face and on the ledges blocked my ears from navigating by sound. It had been hard to maneuver up the ladders dragging one leg when it was dry. Doing it now in the pouring rain was even worse. The minutes dragged long and twice I slipped, barely catching myself, my breath ragged and laced with fear when I'd caught hold more tightly.

At the top of the first ladder, I collapsed in a heap before craning my neck to look upward. Lightning lanced through the sky, lighting the edge of topside. Along the edge, silhouettes stood inky black. My wave was already at the top and I had three more ladders to go. My hands wouldn't stop shaking with fatigue and my good leg ached from doing twice the work. If I slipped on a ladder it would be no different than falling off the dragon. I would fall to my death.

I scanned the cliffside for the bench and pulleys. If I kept relying on the ladder I would be too late. There. It was down along the ledge. I fought my way up to my feet, pushing back exhaustion and fear and scrambled towards the ladder, my crutch slipping and twisting over the wet ground. I stumbled, falling hard onto the ledge, my crutch sailing away.

I lay on the ground for a moment, grateful to have stayed on the ledge and not careened over the side. My cheek was burning with pain and when I felt it with my hand it was tender to the touch. It felt wet, but everything did. I could taste blood in my mouth and my good knee and palms were throbbing. I couldn't let injury stop me. There would be time to tend my wounds after.

I scrambled to my hands and knee and scanned the ledge for my crutch. It was gone. The bottom fell out of my stomach and everything inside me wanted to let loose at once. I turned to the side and heaved, bringing up everything I had, and then wiping my mouth with the back of my hand. I shook my head, gasping in the pouring rain, my body shaking and spasming almost uncontrollably as I drew in the scraps of determination I still had. I needed to be courageous. Yes, this was bad. It could be worse. It could be me who fell over that cliff edge.

The bench wasn't far, so I crawled to it. Slick as it was, venturing onto it felt foolhardy at best, but I swung my good leg over, wrapping that leg around the underside of the board to grip it. I grabbed the rope with both hands, hauling on it like I had before. Wet and heavy, it responded sluggishly, barely moving a few inches instead of the meters it had soared upwards at a single pull before. Despair washed over me. With my crutch gone, this was my last hope. I had to get there with the bench or lose any hope of becoming a Dragon Rider. Tears flowed from my eyes that I didn't bother to hold back, but I heaved on the rope, again, and again, and again until I was sobbing and panting all at once, my palms raw and sore from the wet rope and my arms shaking and wobbly.

There was no way I could make it.

There was no way I could let myself give up.

All this time, in all of my life, I had never given up. If I started now, then I might as well give up on everything, and then what? Should I just die while I was at it? No. I gritted my teeth, closed my eyes and pulled. I was halfway up when I felt a whoosh of wind that was unfamiliar and I looked up. Our dragons were circling in the sky above, Dragon Riders positioned on either end of the train of dragons. Everyone else was about to take their First Flight. If I didn't get up there and take mine, then what would happen to Raolcan?

I pulled, fear and desperation coursing through me, my nose and eyes running freely with a combination of frustration, anger, and despair. Why. Did. It. Always. Seem. To. Happen. To. Me? Why?

Where are you?

I gasped, almost dropping the rope and then clutching it tighter when I realized what I'd almost done. Raolcan! I could hear him again!

The magic of the bonding mutes our voices. We come to you completely vulnerable in that ceremony, without even a voice to speak.

That was horrible! Why would they do that to a sentient creature like Raolcan?

They fear our thoughts. We think differently than they do.

I'm so sorry, Raolcan. I didn't know what to do but I just couldn't walk away from you. I chose to bond with you but it's not my intention to make you a slave.

It's okay, spider. Remember, I chose you.

He did, didn't he? And why did he call me spider?

A private joke. Don't ask.

I didn't have time to ask, anyway. I needed to pull harder. It wasn't just me relying on this, it was Raolcan, too.

What do you need to pull on? Why can't I see you with the others? They're lined up for us.

I'm on the bench trying to get up the side of the cliff. I lost my crutch. If I don't get there in time to ride you then I miss my shot. I won't be your Dragon Rider.

Something lashed out, rocking me mentally, so that I had to grip the rope tight and rest my forehead against it, flinching from the agony. Was that a dragon's mental curse?

Hold tight. I'll find a way to get to you.

A nice thought but he was a slave and if I didn't hurry we'd never see each other again. I set back to work, but a scream pierced the sky and I stopped again, gripping the rope, my gaze darting around looking for the screamer.

I caught sight of him for only a moment as he fell past me, arms and legs pinwheeling through the air. His mouth and eyes wide in terror. Good-looking Jael would never flirt with Starie or Savette again. If I hadn't already lost my dinner, I would now. I bit my lip as my whole body shook, fighting down fear through clenched fists and teeth. The only thing that wouldn't clench tightly was my eyes. Every time I closed them the image of Jael falling past resurfaced.

I didn't look up for the second scream. I didn't want to know who it was. I didn't want to have to remember their face forever.

Chapter Sixteen

MY TEETH CHATTERED and my limbs shook. My muscles were past burning with pain and into a dead zone beyond that. Would they give me any warning before they let go altogether? I didn't dare think about that. I needed to draw on any strength I could find. I took a deep breath, determining to be strong, insisting within myself that I push past my fear and refuse to quit. I must not give in. I would be strong. Above me, thunder crashed so loudly that it left my ears ringing. I risked a glance as lightning pierced the clouds.

White light flooded the sky and I could finally see a string of dragons soaring through the sky. Starie was on hers, hair wild and posture stiff. As I watched, Daedru leapt through the air, landing squarely on the back of his Golden dragon and deftly strapping in. I drew in a deep breath. Despite the storm, not all of my wave were perishing. There were other silhouettes on dragons, but I didn't have time to identify any of them before the thunder boomed again and the light faded away.

A second spear of lightning appeared and in the glow, I saw Savette swinging, half-on and half-off her Red dragon. The dragon was tumbling slowly, like he was trying to keep her on with his movement, but her flailing legs found no purchase and her arms gripped the saddle awkwardly. Had she missed the mount? Had she caught the saddle on the way past?

Why was no one diving towards her? Why was no one helping? If there was ever a time to rush, this was it! Savette couldn't have more than a few minutes before her grip broke and she fell. Raolcan? Can you help? Please, please help her!

The wind intensified, battering at me so that I had to re-double my grip and shut my eyes against the intensity.

Now.

I opened my eyes. What was he talking about?

Below you.

He was there, hovering below me. The pit of my stomach felt like it was dropping through my knees to complete First Flight without me. Here was my chance.

I could do this.

I couldn't do this.

I was frozen. My hands refused to relax and my leg was stiff from clamping so hard around the bench.

I won't drop you.

But Eeamdor had dropped Savette, and those other drag-ons had dropped their people. A bond prevented direct harm but the magic didn't extend to accidents.

Trust me.

How could I trust anyone? There was no one who took care of Amel Leafbrought except Amel Leafbrought.

I will have to trust you, too. After all, you are the one who will command my entire future. The least you can do is entrust your physical safety to me.

If I was going to trust him, then I needed to so it now. A sliver of gold lit the edge of the horizon. Dawn was coming.

Don't make me sorry I chose you.

I couldn't allow myself to listen to the voice in my mind listing all the reasons this was foolishness and demanding that I rethink it all. My only hope was to trust and take the chance. I swung my good leg around so that both legs were free to leap. I let go of the rope with one hand, wiping my sweaty palm on my soaked clothes. I took a deep breath.

Don't think. Don't think. Don't think. Don't close your eyes.

I dropped.

Air rushed past, drying out my open eyes. Everything seemed to slow, as I turned into the fall, belly down, arms thrust before me to lessen the impact when I met him. He was below me, hovering somehow. He seemed too small to land on. What if I missed him? What if I was knocked loose like Savette? My heart was in my throat. Was that me screaming?

Suddenly, he was all I could see. I let myself fall into him, gripping anything I could grab the second my hands found purchase. My face pressed against his scales and my good leg found the stirrup. I needed to sit up and strap in, but he was moving so much: up and down, side to side. I thought I was going to be sick again. He didn't feel firm beneath me. Instead, he bobbed like the ferry on the river, like he was supported by water.

I have to move to compensate for you. You aren't' balancing yourself. Strap in.

I swallowed hard, fear making me whimper a little as I felt with one hand for the strap, my cheek still pressed against his scales. Irrational as it may be, I felt safer pressed against him.

I grabbed the strap and wrapped it single-handed around my waist. The buckle would require two hands. I clenched my teeth hard, gripped the belt with one hand and brought the other around to grip the other side, buckling myself clumsily into the saddle. How did anyone get used to this? The harness slid on easily once the waist strap was bucked and I sat up.

Hold on tight if you want to help your friend.

He dove so suddenly that I cried out, my fingers splayed against his scaly back and my hair rushing behind me. I hadn't bound it back tonight. I should have thought of something but I'd been too worried.

There was the Red dragon, spiraling slowly towards the rocks. Savette still struggled, trying to pull herself into the saddle but her movements lacked the vigor of earlier. She was losing the fight. They were both going down. Raolcan's dive was so fast it was almost magical, and then he changed the shape of his wings so they were cupping the air and we slowed to settle beside the Red dragon. He tipped to one side, bringing me close to Savette as he moved his wings in a complicated pattern that kept us hovering beside the other dragon. Something was wrong with Eeamdor's reins. He was tangled in them. That explained some of the problem.

I locked gazes with Savette and her eyes were so wide I thought she must not even see me.

"Grab my hand!" I held it out to her, but she didn't dare take it. If only Raolcan could get us closer. And then we were – as he read my thoughts. He dipped a little lower and I grabbed Savette around the waist, pushing her upward until she could scramble into the saddle. She belted in as I worked on Eeamdor's knotted reins.

"I don't know how they tangled. I was leaping and then he was hurt." She sounded rattled, and no wonder.

Get him free fast. We're running out of time.

The rocks below us were growing closer as we fell, Eeamdor still too enmeshed to right himself. There wasn't time to sort out the tangled mess.

Knife. In my saddle. Standard equipment.

I felt the edge of the saddle and found a stiff leather pouch, opening it hastily and losing a fabric parcel and a flint as I searched desperately for the knife. There it was. I heard a clatter below us as my abandoned items hit the rocks below. Desperately, I sawed at Eeamdor's reigns. One cut through. The next cut.

We swooped upward, the Red flying with us, free of his entanglement.

We did it. I breathed a sigh of relief. They were safe.

And I was flying. I hadn't even had a chance to enjoy it yet. Every bump and swell still put my heart in my throat but exhilaration filled me. I could almost have flown all on my own. No one who did this should be a slave. Certainly not Raolcan.

I trust you, Raolcan.

I trust you, Spider.

Along the horizon, the sun slipped up like it was just a normal day. The clouds of the storm were interspersed with bright blue sky and everything was so wet that it glowed gold in the light of dawn. Something about a dawn made the horrors of the night feel distant. Maybe they were. Maybe I'd end my First Flight to discover that the things I'd seen weren't what I thought they were. I hoped so, but in this moment, I wasn't thinking about that. I was thinking about what it felt like to fly.

Because it was for this that I'd been born and whatever came after could never take this away from me.

From us, Raolcan echoed and I knew that was true - knew it deep to my core. I wasn't alone in this journey anymore.

READ MORE OF AMEL LEAFBROUGHT'S story in Dragon School: Initiate.[1]

Behind the Scenes:

USA TODAY BESTSELLING author, Sarah K. L. Wilson, hails from the rocky Canadian Shield in Northern Ontario where she lives with her husband and two small boys. Her interests include the outdoors, history, and philosophy. Her books are always about fantastical adventures in other worlds.

Sarah would like to thank **Harold Trammel** and **Sarah Brown** for their incredible work in beta reading and proofreading this book. Without their big hearts and passion for stories, this book would not be the same.

Join Sarah's mailing list[1] for news about her books.

Visit Sarah's **website**[2] for a complete list of available titles.

FACEBOOK[3] | INSTAGRAM[4] | TWITTER[5]

---

1.   http://hyperurl.co/newslettersignup

2.   http://www.sarahklwilson.com

3.   https://www.facebook.com/sarahklwilson

4.   https://www.instagram.com/sarahklwilson/

5.   https://twitter.com/sarah_kl_wilson

Made in the USA
San Bernardino, CA
17 November 2018